ndrej Nikolaidis is a contemporary writer from one of Europe's newest and smallest states: Montenegro. He is also a polemical journalist whose writing is fundamental to the process of democratic dialogue in the region. He has written three novels and was awarded the European Prize for Literature 2011.

THE COMING

Andrej Nikolaidis

Translated from the Montenegrin by Will Firth

First published in 2012
by Istros Books
London, United Kingdom
www.istrosbooks.com

Chapter One of *The Coming* was first published in *Best European Fiction
2012*, Dalkey Archive Press, Champaign/Dublin/London, 2011

Typeset by CB editions, London
Printed in England by ImprintDigital, Exeter EX5 5HY

Cover photo and design: Roxana Stere

The right of Andrej Nikolaidis to be identified as the author
of this work has been asserted in accordance with the Copyright,
Designs and Patents Act, 1988

ISBN 978-1-90823-6036

This edition has been made possible with the help of the Ministry of
Culture of Montenegro.

Education and Culture DG

Culture Programme

This project has been funded with support from the European Commission.
This publication reflects the views only of the author, and the Commission
cannot be held responsible for any use which may be made of the information
contained therein.

The Messiah will come only when he is no longer necessary; he will come only on the day after his arrival; he will come, not on the last day, but at the very last.

– Franz Kafka

The world clearly constitutes a single system, i.e., a coherent whole, but the knowledge of this system presupposes a knowledge of all nature and history, which man will never attain. Hence he who makes systems must fill in the countless gaps with figments of his own imagination, i.e., engage in irrational fancies, ideologise.

– Friedrich Engels

Chapter Seven

Chapter Eight

Chapter Nine

THE COMING

Chapter One

which tells of a gruesome crime, anger, snow and the corruptness of human nature

*T*he smell of blood reached us even before we entered the house, yet there were no signs of a break-in at the front door. Clearly the murderer had rung the bell and a member of the household had opened up for him. I turned around to Yanko:

'Perhaps it was someone they knew.'

'Psssht!' he hissed, probably afraid the murderer was still in the house.

I looked back. Curious neighbours were already clustering around our patrol car behind the row of cypresses which skirted the Vukotić' property. Some kids were roaring down the road in a souped-up yellow Fiat with music blaring and almost lost control at the bend. They spotted the crowd, slowed down, and drove back.

'Turn that off,' someone yelled at them, 'there's been a murder here!'

I forced the door with my shoulder and took a step into the house, gripping my pistol as tightly as I could, with both hands. It felt cold, as if I'd just picked it up out of the snow. Yanko came in behind me and lit the way with his flashlight. We heard a movement in the dark, or at least we thought we

3

did, but it was hard to tell. We were on edge. Terrified, to tell the truth. It was my first murder, after all. Sure, I'd seen a lot of corpses before, but I don't think any sane person can get used to death.

When we heard the noise, or thought we did, Yanko flashed his light into the kitchen. I stepped forward, ready to shoot. Then my legs caught on something and I fell. My cheek was warm and wet. 'Fuck this,' I called, 'turn on the light.'

I was lying in Senka Vukotić's blood. I found some paper towels in the kitchen and wiped my face and hands, while Yanko photographed Senka.

'I think I moved her,' I told him.

There was a large wound on her head. It turned out that the murderer had dealt the first blow with an axe. Evidently that didn't kill her outright, so he knelt down and cut her throat. We didn't find the knife, but the axe is at the lab in Podgorica for analysis.

The trail of blood led to the internal staircase. The lab later reported that the murderer had been wearing size seven gumboots with worn-out soles. As soon as he set foot on the stairs, Pavle must have fired at him: two shots, we found the buckshot in the wall. It's incredible that he didn't hit him. We combed the house several times but couldn't find any trace of the murderer's blood. That's what fear does to you – Pavle was firing from above, from the top of the stairs, at a distance of no more than five yards. But before he could reload the shotgun the murderer was upon him. From what we've been able to reconstruct, it seems the first blow struck Pavle in the right shoulder. As the murderer swung the axe again to deal the mortal blow, Pavle dashed off into the bathroom and tried to hide.

But what happened next makes us certain that the murderer knew the family and had been to the house before: instead of going after Pavle he went into the children's room. He knew they had children – that's the point – and he knew where to find them. He grabbed Sonja in the bed by the window. She was seven, Jesus Christ . . . One blow was enough for a small child like that.

Meanwhile, Pavle realised he'd left the children at the tender mercies of the murderer. He ran into their room and found the intruder on the floor – the killer had needed to set down the axe to grab Helena, who'd hidden under her bed. That was the second chance Pavle had that night. He didn't get a third. Although he now had the axe, which put him at a clear advantage, the murderer overpowered him and cut his throat, like he did with Senka down in the hall.

Helena tried to run away but she didn't get far. We found her body in the living room, on the couch in front of the television, which was still on. Judging by the bloodstains, the murderer sat down next to her. Our psychologists are trying to unravel what that could possibly mean. One thing's for sure – he switched on Animal Planet.

Then he left. No one saw him, no one heard him, and he left no fingerprints or DNA. There won't be any further investigations because, as I'm sure you know, homeless people laid waste to the house and ultimately set it on fire.

Quite a story, don't you think? I reckon you've got something for your two hundred euros! Inspector Jovanović exclaimed.

'You can say that again!' I said, patting him on the shoulder. I ordered a beer for him, paid, and went outside. But I didn't get very far. Each day I went back to the pub, sat

5

behind the same sticky bar and listened to the same story like a bloody refrain I couldn't get out of my head.

*

I remembered all that again as I sat in a long line of cars that evening and stared at the fire-blackened ruins of the library covered with snow. It was like a white sheet spread over a dead body: although it conceals the body underneath, everyone knows there's been a crime.

I was beginning to realise that I'd need at least an hour to get out of that traffic jam. It was cold that night, and the snow had turned to ice because there was no one to clear it off the roads. A driver had probably failed to brake on time and crashed into the car in front, and even on an evening like that they managed to get into a fight about it. The police were already on their way to restore order. I could see the blue rotating lights through the snow which was now falling ever more thickly. Luckily, I'd filled up before the Ulcinj petrol station closed and all the staff were sent home. I heard that when the petrol station ran dry, they rang the head office in Kotor to ask for another tankload. They called all morning, and finally around noon they got through to someone. The fellow told them everything was over – no one needed anything now, least of all petrol. 'I mean, what are people going to do with it? It's not like they can escape,' he said, his voice thick with depression. He complained that his wife had kicked him out of the house. She'd told him to get lost – she at least wanted to die without having him around. And with nowhere else to go, he simply went back to the office. There wasn't another living soul at the Hellenic Petroleum depot. When the workers at the petrol station finally realised that the end of the world also meant they'd lose their jobs, they divided up the money in the till. The gas cylinders they'd sold to customers in happier times were now heaved into the boots of their cars, and plastic bags full of sweets, cigarettes and bottles of whisky were crammed into the back seats. They didn't bother to lock the door when they left. Now they're probably guzzling down Chivas Regal and their children are gorging themselves sick on sweets to make sure nothing will be left. Like they say, it's a shame to waste things.

The fuel gauge under the speedometer told me I had enough petrol for all I needed to do that evening. The motor rumbled reliably. I turned up the heating and put in a new CD. Odawas sang 'Alleluia' while several men with long black beards marched past in formation. They were rushing to the mosque because it was time for prayer. The lights on the minarets blinked like a lighthouse. But it's too late now, I brooded, we're still going to hit the rocks. You can crawl under the red altars, run into the minarets – slender rockets ready to take you away to a different world – but it will be as promised: tonight, no one will be able to hide.

That night warranted an update of all our dictionaries, if only there had been time, so as to add the definitive new meaning of '*dead*line': everything anyone in the world still planned to do had to be done that night. Working under pressure? I was used to it, even though I initially imagined that being a private detective in a town as small and peaceful as Ulcinj would be safe and easy. Cheated husbands, suspicious wives – who could need my services apart from unhappy people in unhappy marriages? That's what I thought, at least.

*

When I first rented an office in the centre of town I furnished it minimally but tastefully, by anyone's standards. Posters of classic old movies went up on the walls: *The Maltese Falcon* with Humphrey Bogart, *Chinatown* with Jack Nicholson . . . The posters were to discreetly prompt clients to compare me with the best. A little pretentious, I admit, but it proved effective. A massive oaken desk dominated the room. Period furniture was installed to give clients the impression they were engaging a company with traditional standards – and people still believe in tradition, although tradition always betrays them if they don't betray it first. The desk sported a black Mercedes typewriter: a real antique and pure extravagance. I wanted everyone who came in to know that we didn't allow any newfangled gadgets like computers in the firm. I wanted clients to know that our methods were time-tested. A detective needs to seem timeless. I wanted people to think: wow, this is a hard-boiled, old-school detective who can be a real tough guy where necessary; a Sam Spade type of character who's seen a lot and knows the mean streets but isn't afraid to jump back into the thick of things if circumstances require.

As soon as I opened my agency, though, it seems all of Ulcinj decided to start killing, robbing, abducting and raping. And there was plenty of adultery too: it must be close to a dozen marriages I've torn apart. I'll always remember those jobs most fondly, given the rest of my blood-soaked career.

I follow the adulterers to their hotel, make myself comfortable in my car, and knock back a swig or two of whisky – just enough to give them time to undress and get down to business. A few photographs as evidence, and the matter is settled. My own experience in such matters is rather scant, I should say, or at least not as extensive as I'd have liked it to be, but one thing's for certain – women cope with adultery much better. A woman sees her partner's adultery as a betrayal: she's angry and offended. But a man who's just found out his wife is cheating on him sees it as a humiliation and irrefutable proof that he's not man enough. When a woman finds out she's been cheated on, her femininity is abruptly heightened. It's as if she has a 'femininity switch' which her husband inadvertently activates by having an affair. But a cheated man crumples like a used condom. Little in this world is as fragile as masculinity – I've learned that lesson well.

Another thing which quickly became clear to me: whether I'm solving *serious crimes* like murder or *crimes of the heart* (as one romantically inclined and, to my delight, promiscuous lady client once described adultery), the most important thing is to understand *what the client wants*. The ones who hire me to find out if their partner is cheating on them thirst for evidence that their suspicions are justified. If a wife is cheating on her husband, she's a bitch; if she isn't cheating on him, he's a swine for suspecting her. Faced with the choice between a negative image of her and a negative image of himself, he always chooses the former. Each of us obviously has unlimited potential for swinishness. Whether and in what form that potential comes out is just a minor technical detail. So I always make a point of presenting extensive evidence of adultery – a photomontage works wonders, irrespective of whether the said adultery actually took place. If it didn't, it still could have, so in a way I'm communicating a deeper truth. And after all, the client comes first. If the client is satisfied, my own satisfaction is assured.

Things are more complicated with murder. To generalise a little, I'd say there are two kinds of murder-investigation clients: those who want to know *who* committed the murder, and those who want to know *why*. With the latter it's easy: you have a chat with them. When they drop in to inquire how the investigation's going, you invite them down to a local bar . . . people loosen up after a drink. Sooner or later they'll give you a hint as to their suspicions, and then the case is as good as cracked. From then on you just confirm the story they themselves have come up with. Tell them you're close to solving the case, but make them wait a little longer. For some reason people consider what they call *arriving at the truth* to be a thankless job. *The truth is a hard road*, several clients have said.

But those who want to know *who* the murderer was are hard to please. They usually want to take revenge, so you can't just point a finger at the first passer-by. It usually ends up that after trying to resolve the case for a while, I give up, cancel the contract and just ask them to cover my expenses.

The way people think is to a detective's advantage. Tell them any old story and they'll exclaim: *I knew it!* Whatever tale you tell, even if it's got as many holes as Swiss cheese, people will say: *Yes, it's logical!* There's evidence for everything – all you need is a story to back it up. By way of illustration, let's take the World Cup football final. A penalty shoot-out will decide who gets to be world champion. The last shot is taken by the best player on the planet. Whether he scores or misses, people will say: I knew it! Because it's *logical* that the best player will score when it's hardest, just as it's *logical* that the best player will miss in a decisive moment because, as we know, fate is often unkind.

My point is that a detective's work isn't so much about finding out the truth as inventing a story which people will accept as the truth. It's not about discovering the truth but about discovering what truth is for those people. Truth always appears as a fiction and takes the form of a story. I am a storyteller.

*

Still stuck in the un-moving traffic, I looked back on my detective career and remembered when the first of the e-mails arrived which caused my *grand illusion* to collapse . . . Funnily enough, around that time I found myself in a similar situation to now: caught in a long line of cars after leaving Inspector Jovanović with his beer and his inability to accept that the massacre he'd described for me did actually happen. Fortunately, this inability didn't prevent him from selling me the information. The massacre at the Vukotićs' would always be an 'incident' for him – something which happened despite the fact that things like that don't happen. Or always happen to someone else. I believe we're able to overlook the horror of our own lives, and we owe our strength to that blindness. Lies are all that liberate us: one drop of the truth would be enough to destroy what remains of our life.

I remember it was feeling every bit of 40 degrees centigrade that day, and the wind had turned into a dry sirocco from North Africa. The fishermen, who sleep with radios close to their ears, had hauled their boats up onto the sand the night before. Ulcinj doesn't have a marina, so an accurate weather forecast and quick legs are all that saves their boats from the waves determined to smash them on the rocks. Radio Dubrovnik got it right again yesterday: the sea did rise after midnight.

It was as if someone had created a vacuum over the town. Everything under the sky was gasping for breath. I searched for a whiff of fresh air in the park across from the pub. Then I went up to the bar: a whisky with two ice cubes. All in vain: wherever I went I breathed in the heat. It was as if the world had turned into an oven which was open right in front of my face and I was leaning into it. But isn't it like that with every change: we decide on it not *because of* things, but *despite* them?

All the local schizophrenics were out on the streets that day – drinking Coca Cola, ranting, smoking as they walked, and often changing pace and direction as if they didn't know where they were going, making them indistinguishable from tourists. The town was full of people whose diagnosis was unknown but whose condition obviously required immediate hospitalisation.

A little later I found myself driving through a horde of tourists: moving like a herd of animals heading to a watering hole. That's how they go down the steep Ulcinj streets to the beach, knocking over and trampling everything in their path. They walk right down the middle of the road because it's wider than the pavement, so they can move faster, and speed is important because it allows them to occupy a spot on the beach closer to the water. They don't move to the side when a car comes – experience has taught them that the driver won't run them over. They don't react to the honk of horns and don't comprehend verbal abuse.

I saw on television that farmers in America have jeeps with rubber grille guards. The driver just drives straight ahead and anything in the way gets pushed aside. The vehicle doesn't injure the animals but directs the movement of the herd. Give a little gas, and then it's just straight ahead. *Go West,* eh? But America is far, far away. For someone who's decided to go to the pine forest today and get nicely drunk amid the pinecones and the scent of resin, the mistral and the shade, the problem is not just the pedestrians, not just the tourists – his *fellow citizens* are enough of a calamity. The ones with cars are the worst: they have driver's licences, names, surnames and even biographies. They have everything except regard for other human beings.

People can rein in their desires. They really expect little of life. Simple things count – like getting in the car and driving to where there's lots of whisky and ice. But however little we desire, we end up getting even less. I sat and waited in a line of cars hundreds of metres long. People were hot and edgy. They sounded their horns, some cursed and swore, others were calm because the priests had taught them to accept fate (another word for chaos). After one or two minutes which seemed like one or two hours, the line gradually got moving again like a giant snake. I know from experience that when there's a traffic jam in Ulcinj it's always because of some brain-dead neanderthal stopping and talking with another driver, or because he's parked in the middle of the road so he can go into a betting shop. We passed the culprit of that day's stoppage: a square-headed young guy with a look of vacant stupidity who had stopped in front of the bakery and blocked the lane leading down to Mala Plaža beach. He ordered a pizza from his car and waited for it to be made and brought to him. Then he didn't have the right change, so he waited – meaning *we* waited – for the assistant to go and fetch change for a twenty-euro note. All this was done without any hurry, with the greatest philosophical composure, paying no heed to the other people and cars, to the heat and the horns blaring . . . like a cow in serene Zen meditation – for only cows on the road manifest quite the same indifference toward the surrounding world, a tranquillity and resolve to do the first thing which comes into their heads: usually to dump a load of dung right where they're standing.

A person's degree of primitivism in an urban setting can be gauged by his indifference toward other people and their needs, by the firmness of his conviction that he's alone in the world and has a right to do whatever he wants here and now, regardless of the misfortune it may cause other people. His place is in *nature*. There he learned that to exist means to mistreat. He's unburdened by the illusions of *Homo urbanus* – for him nature is not a delicate equilibrium, a sensitive and complex organism; nature has only mistreated him and his tribe throughout history, harassing them with droughts, storms, floods, and frosts; they've fled from nature and have brought nothing but nature with them because they *are* nature. A person's degree of primitivism in an urban setting can

14

be gauged, I maintain, by the disturbance he represents for other people. A primitive person is unable to exist in quiet discretion: he always creates noise, unsightliness, and stench. He does everything he can to be noticed – he constantly *emits* his existence. His being is a blow to the senses and an insult to the intelligence. He mistreats us with his very existence. When he celebrates, a considerate, tasteful person unfortunate enough to live next door to him is bound to suffer. What a primitive person enjoys inflicts pain on the civilised.

I read in the paper about an Austrian in Vienna who shot his Bosnian neighbour. It turned out that the Bosnian had driven the Austrian out of his mind for years with the loud Balkan folk music which he listened to in his apartment every afternoon. The Austrian complained to the police several times, and they intervened in accordance with the law, but that didn't prevent the Bosnian from continuing to mistreat the Austrian. When he realised that all legal possibilities of protecting his calm and privacy had been exhausted, the Austrian shot the Bosnian in the head and calmly turned himself in to the police.

That story stuck in my mind because it tells us that the law can't protect us from the primitive, who is nothing but a walking disaster. However brutal the law is, it can't compare with the brutality of nature. When law is about revenge, as in the case of capital punishment, it's closest to nature – and thus furthest from the law.

That's why it's so unbearable here: primitivism is not some random excess but the very *essence* of local culture, which therefore isn't a culture. If you're not primitive here you're a foreign body and you'll be made to feel it every day. With a lot of effort, luck and money you can construct a fortress and preserve your own order of things inside it – for a while. You can erect high walls, dig moats and build drawbridges to shut off your world *for a while*. But they'll find a way in: like in Poe's 'Masque of the Red Death', their *nature* will get through and wipe your little world off the face of the earth.

Here people dump garbage by the roadside and turn the landscape into a landfill. Their sheep and goats, which they need in order to survive in their suburbs, wander the asphalt and graze the parks, or what's left of them. Their children imitate the cherubs in fancy fountains and pee in flowerbeds in front of the passers-by. They shit on the beaches and in neglected recreation centres. Music is the form of art they like most because it doesn't demand interpretation or reflection. Like the salt strewn on a vanquished ancient city they sow the world with noise – repulsive music lasting late into the night is what they need in order to enjoy themselves. Walls and billboards are plastered with pictures of their big-titted women with frightening faces and grimaces which we can only assume are meant to suggest lust but which actually attest to nothing but stupidity and vacuousness. The males of the species thrust their ever-erect organs into that void, and from that nothingness *their* children are born to ensure the continuation of *their* world, nation, family and culture – of *their* kind.

There are times like that day, stuck amid all those people, every one of them a nerve-grating nuisance, when anger grips me so tightly that no insult I could ever think of and no salvo of sarcasm I could fire at their civilians – their women and children – could bring relief. Those are times when anger grips me so tightly that I can't move, as if the black monolith from *2001* was weighing down on my chest, times when anger is all that exists – when I'm anger itself. Then I think: death. What comes next has to be death. If there's anything after and beyond anger, it can only be that. Those were my thoughts that day as I nestled into my car seat, gripped the steering wheel – and waited.

It's fascinating that something as dependable as death becomes so utterly unreliable if we dare to count on it for release, because as a rule it arrives too late. The only mitigating circumstance is that, because it takes its time in coming, we're never truly disappointed. They say that *Homo sapiens* are animals endowed with reason. I'd say that, despite this reason, they're animals punished with optimism. Because as soon as the pistol is removed from their forehead, the boot lifted from their neck and the blade pulled from their belly, they think: things will get better. But before they can even cross themselves and pronounce *faith, hope and love* a few times, they'll be cast face-down in the mud again, and then death won't seem so terrible and unfair.

Nope, not this time either – everything's as it was before, I said to myself, and noticed that the people around me were starting to get out of their cars. They raised their eyes to the sky, called out to one another, seized their heads in their hands, and spread out their arms in wonder. Then the first flake fell on the windscreen. I opened the window and peered out: as serene and dignified as a Hollywood White Christmas, snow fell on Ulcinj that June day.

Chapter Two

*in which the snow continues to fall, we meet good Hedvige and
old Marcus, and stroll with Emmanuel from Schikanedergasse to
Naschmarkt*

from: emmanuel@gmail.com
to: thebigsleep@yahoo.com

Even here, in this room where I'm confined – *for my own good*,
they never fail to say – the first snow brings serenity and joy.
And even though the narrow slice of landscape I see through
the window is now my whole world, that world is sublime in its
beauty once it's covered in white. The west wind casts snow
on the gnarled branches of the plum tree, the browning grass
of the hill and the bristling willows. There are other days when
the lake is a leaden grey and impossible to distinguish from
the sky, which is eternally grey here in the Alps. The surface of
the water sometimes shakes as if someone were walking on
it, unseen and unheard. The water ripples and the little waves
move towards me. They won't shake the willow branches dip-
ping into the lake and don't have the strength to reach the
shore. If it weren't for me patiently awaiting them every winter
as I stare out through the window, probably no one would notice their so potent existence.

Those waves which won't foam, let alone carry away or

smash anything, are a sign: they herald the first snow. The wind which raised them will soon strengthen and bring driving snow to the lake. A flurry of snowflakes will descend on the landscape and white will re-establish its order. But not before several large, watery stars have stuck to my window. By evening, ice will have covered the glass: I'll press my face up against it and feel the cold on my forehead. Outside everything is at rest, and inside everyone has fallen asleep. That is my time: I can melt the ice with my breath right through until morning. Every few seconds I breathe life into a shape – and a being on the window-pane starts to move. Now it's a bird, next time it's a wolf. And however often the cold comes for them and the ice reclaims them, I bring them back with my breath.

My world lacks breadth, perhaps. It lacks people, above all, because apart from the village children in summer who go scooting down the grassy hillside on sheets of cardboard and plunge head-first into the lake with a scream – hardly anyone calls by. But there's no lack of order. My world is as ordered as a Chekhov play. If I mention a plum tree, children will come and pick its fruit in the autumn. If I look at the willows, some youngster is bound to jump from them into the water by the end of the summer to demonstrate his manliness, which in my world and all others is always done in primitive and superfluous ways. And then there's the lake! It, too, is a nail which someone will hang their coat on by the end of the play. Its waters are calm and buoyant, it accepts visitors . . . and sometimes keeps the particularly careless and weak. As I say, there's no lack of order in my world. Nor any lack of excitement: there are quite enough changes for my liking.

Not to mention memories. When you're confined, you learn to live backwards. Tomorrow will be the same as today. The only future you have is your memory. The only uncertainty which awaits you is what you'll remember tomorrow. You go back and tell yourself stories in which you're the main hero. Most of those stories never happened, but who cares – they could have happened, and that's all that counts. Your past contains innumerable possibilities for lives different to the one you live. So: go back, young man!

I go back to the hall of our Vienna apartment in 5 Schikanedergasse. I'm seven years old. From my hiding place behind the shoe cabinet I can see that my nanny has fallen asleep in the armchair beneath Lucian Freud's painting. The picture had belonged to our neighbour who committed suicide after the bank took away all his property, but not before *papa* bought the picture from him 'for a fair and reasonable price', as he and my mother emphasised every time Freud was the topic of conversation in our drawing room. Fair and reasonable wasn't good enough for the bank, which confiscated and flogged off all the neighbour's possessions, turning the heir of a tailor's shop which had *clothed the Viennese for over three centuries* into a homeless pauper who had no choice but to drown himself in the Danube, a way in which people in a similar quandary had ended their lives for more than three centuries.

So Hedvige, my nanny, was sleeping beneath the picture painted by the grandson of the great dream interpreter. My parents had gone to visit Aunt Esther, who'd been dying for at least as long as I'd been alive. When they took me to see her the first time, she was lying like a big white polar bear on a wide, heavy bed, the same one I found her on when we'd visited the last time, at New Year. When they introduced me to Aunt Esther, she said: 'The boy is most irritatingly blue-eyed – I can't help it, but those misty blue eyes have something distinctly Prussian about them.'

Three paces and I was at the front door, which I closed behind me noiselessly. A descent down the wide, marble stair-case awaited me. The stairs were made so that they not tire a person out. *Papa* always made a point of emphasising what he called 'the humaneness of Vienna's stairs'. I don't think we ever went up to our apartment together without him remarking that these stairs could teach you all you needed to know about Viennese architecture. Although it mirrored the narcissism of tradition and the power of the former empire, it above all re-flected the idea that 'buildings, even the most palatial ones, are to serve people' – I think those were his words. To his mind, Viennese stairs had to be made so that walking up them was no more strenuous than a Sunday stroll on Stephans-platz. Vienna's opera houses were the only buildings on the planet fit to host operas: everything else was a barbaric blas-phemy which ought to be banned by law. The proportion of the height of the ceiling to the length of the windows in Vien-nese cafés was simply perfect, and visitors got the impression they were drinking their *kleiner Brauner* in the very centre of the world. Overpriced Parisian cafés were claustrophobic and kind of obscure, *papa* claimed. The cafés in Rome, on the other hand, seemed frivolous: when you were drinking your espresso there you felt the visitors and waiters were about to tear off their civilian clothes or uniforms and show themselves in costumes, revealing their true nature as characters from a commedia dell'arte. In a nutshell: *papa* loved Vienna, and a life outside that city was unimaginable for him.

The stairs which were made so that even the oldest residents of Vienna, at least those who were still mobile, could mount them with a minimum of effort, were also made so that I could imitate the hops of a kangaroo – the animal which fascinated me most at the time – and go bounding down them two steps at a time without danger of falling and getting hurt, although I doubt that was the intention of the constructors. When I'd jumped the last few steps, it was just four more hops to the main door of the house. One more after that and I'd finally be out on the snow-covered pavement, staring at the bright sign on the other side of the street: *Carlton Opera Hotel.*

I was a sickly child. If my chronic bronchitis improved for just a second, I'd be bed-ridden with sinus pain. There was probably no day I didn't have a cough, a sore throat or an annoying cold. To top it all off, there were the allergies. I wasn't allowed to eat strawberries: just a morsel of the red fruit sufficed to cause an attack of asphyxiation. We also discovered under dramatic circumstances that I was allergic to penicillin. I was two at the time. After I'd been given an injection of penicillin an intensive red appeared, starting at the point of the injection. Then my temperature shot up, and it took them days to get it to come down again. Just when *maman et papa* had given up hope for me, my fever subsided, and the doctors wrote CAVE PENICILLIN in thick red letters on my medical record card.

What I want to say is that I wasn't allowed to play most children's games. Running out into the snow in only a jumper – without my fur coat, cap and gloves – was a blatant violation of the unwritten but no less rigid rules. It was always the same: I'd use my parents' absence for my street adventures. I'd always return home before they did. Poor Hedvige would be waiting for me in tears after having woken up, called for me, looked in all the hiding places in the apartment, and then burst into inconsolable sobs. It meant nothing to her that I came back running every time: she seemed not to perceive the pattern behind such simple repetition. She'd always be worried out of her mind as if I'd run away for the very first time. She waited for me on the landing at the apartment door, beside herself with anxiety. Instead of scolding me when I returned, she'd lift me up a little, embrace me and repeat: 'Oh Master Emmanuel, thank goodness you've come back to me.' That woman is up with the angels now, I'm sure. 'Don't worry, I won't say a word to *monsieur et madame*,' she'd tell me. She demanded only one thing of me – precisely the one thing I couldn't promise her, however sincerely I regretted the misdemeanours I'd committed each time: *that I never, never do it again*, she repeated in the tone of voice I imagined Heidi's grandfather used to tell her important lessons. And sure enough, she never gave me away. But *I* would go up to *maman et papa* while they were still taking their coats off and admit everything. 'This child is beyond our help,' my mother would sigh and start to cry. 'May God protect you because I obviously can't,' she sobbed and withdrew into her room, complaining of a headache.

Papa would tell Hedvige to give me a warm wash and put me to bed. Later he'd sit on the edge of my bed until I fell asleep and tell me in a low voice, like a lullaby, how much my mother had suffered because of me. It wasn't good to return her kindness like this, he whispered. I felt warmth washing over me, my limbs became as light as wings and I sank into sleep, with his gentle, patient voice a distant echo in my ears: *She's made so many sacrifices for you. She'd do anything for you . . .*

Whenever I was outside, opposite the Carlton Opera Hotel, an irresistible adventure would begin. There was a story connected with that hotel which probably all nannies in the neighbourhood told to give the children a fright. I heard it from Hedvige: *A horrible man hung himself in the hotel. He'd done terrible things during the war many years before you were born. The army he commanded was defeated. But, being cunning, he dyed his hair black, grew a beard and moustache to conceal his identity, donned glasses, changed his name – and disappeared. For ever, people thought. Until one day a woman happened to go and see a doctor who practised in an apartment on the top floor of the Carlton Opera Hotel. She realised it was the same evil man whose hospital she'd been detained at during the war. She called the police and demanded they immediately arrest the doctor, whom she blamed for the death of her husband and thousands of other innocent people. The horrible man probably knew what was in store for him when he saw the police car pull up in front of the hotel. The police called on him and demanded that he give himself up. In the end they broke into his surgery and found him hanging from a light fixture, dressed in the uniform he'd worn during the war. Boys like you mustn't go there because the ghost of the doctor still haunts the halls of the hotel. They say that if he finds children who go there despite the warning, he lures them into the lift with sweets. The lift is like a cage: its doors clang shut and he takes them straight down to hell.* That's what Hedvige used to tell me.

I entered the hotel and saw the terrible lift. Just a few steps lay between me and that shaft to hell. To the left was the reception desk, which was always staffed by several pretty and friendly young women. They knew me by now and called out: 'It's you, Emmanuel! How is the little Master today?' I'd cautiously go up to the desk, raise my hand in greeting and lay it on the marble top. That was part of my rescue strategy: if the doctor appeared in front of me, I counted on the young receptionists whisking me behind the desk. I'd stand there for a while looking at the lift: it was an imposing contraption with thick, black bars and glass which definitely fitted the part. When one of the guests got in, the bars closed behind them and the lift would head upwards with a creak of chains. But when I heard the lift coming down, I'd think it was the evil doctor coming for me. Fear would get the better of my curiosity and I'd turn tail and bolt from the hotel.

I'd run until my cough made me stop. But I didn't go back home. No way, my adventure had only just begun! I'd turn into the first street on the right and stand in front of the windows of old Marcus's shop. There were bottles of liquor with colourful labels – I liked the green ones best, which looked as if they had nothing but smoke in them. More interesting still, Marcus's window displayed a whole range of chocolate bars from exotic parts of the world. *Brazil*, it said, *five, five*, and then a funny sign. *Ecuador, six, five*, and the funny sign again, and *South Africa, Kenya*, and again numbers with signs I didn't understand . . . There outside that luxury food shop, which after Marcus's death was turned into a kebab outlet, I learned that everything I don't know or don't have can be substituted by things I imagine and believe in. There was no chocolate taster for whom those delicacies were more real than for me. Experts could try a little cube of chocolate with their eyes closed and unerringly identify its origin and the class of the cocoa, but what was that compared to the stories I could tell about those chocolates? I trembled with excitement at the yellow, green and orange wrappers with little maps of the countries from which these chocolates arrived in my world: on pack-horses through the jungle, on rafts through foaming rapids, in seaplanes through clouds and storms, on ocean-going ships past icebergs and waves as tall as the Staatsoper . . . The wrappers also showed palm trees, whose fronds the natives used to make huts to shelter from the tropical rain; I saw lions, black women with long necks carrying wicker baskets on their heads, and to top it all off there were stern warriors with spears and blowguns which fired poisoned darts deadlier than the fangs of a cobra; I convinced myself that every thought and word was true.

I'd stand there in front of the shop window until Marcus, who was forever sitting behind the counter reading, looked up through his glasses with lenses as thick as the jars in Hedvige's pantry. Then he'd come hobbling up to the door and pull me inside. 'You've come out without your woollens again,' he'd reproach me, 'you'll be in bed with fever again for a whole month!' And before I could say a word in my defence he'd slip a hot cup of tea into my hand.

His shop always smelt of cinnamon and tobacco. Gentle music was playing which I'd recognise years later as Bach, whom my friend prized above all other composers. Business was going from bad to worse, so Marcus smoked most of the luxury cigars himself when their use-by date expired. He'd blow out the smoke of a thick cigar and say to me, imitating black-and-white-film icons: *When you take poison, you have to do it with style,* a lesson even Socrates read to humanity. Alas, in vain.

Marcus wasn't a man of many words. If I tried to ask him something, he'd reach me one of the books he kept under the counter and say with a crafty smile: *Here, read this*, only to return to his cigar, book and silence. When I'd drunk my tea, and I made sure not to hurry, he'd see me out and send me on my way: 'And now straight home!'

Later, when I was at high school, Hedvige told me that Marcus had sold the shop and used the money to pay for a place in a retirement home in Aspern, on the outskirts of Vienna. Since he had neither children nor any close relatives to look after him, he thought it was the best way of providing for a peaceful retirement. Before leaving our area for good, he met Hedvige on her way back from shopping and asked after me, although I hadn't dropped into his shop for years. He told Hedvige that he'd lived in Aspern throughout the Soviet occupation. After the Russians shot his father in 1946, he grew up with his grandfather there. *'The old man's reign of terror was no better than the Russians'*, he told Hedvige, who then told me. Marcus also mentioned that his father lay in a shallow grave in Aspern, as well as his grandfather, who had maltreated him as long as he'd had a breath left in his body; there were other gruesome memories, too, which he hadn't been able to lay to rest and put behind him. Since that's how things were, he felt it was only right that he also be buried in Aspern when his time came. And with that he politely said goodbye and headed off down the street, leaving a trail of smoke; I can just picture him with his cigar, like an old steamboat proudly chuffing away on its last voyage, to the salvagers.

I didn't go to visit him. Not out of laziness or because I didn't care about him. On the contrary: because he was so important to me. Marcus had known he mustn't give me any of the chocolates from his shop window, however often I came, because that would ruin everything: our little game, all my reveries about faraway countries which began at his shop window, and our whole delicate and sincere friendship. And I knew I mustn't go and see Marcus in the nursing home: he wouldn't be behind the counter, on the throne of his empire, but enfeebled in a bed or wheelchair. No, it was best this way: kind old Marcus would forever stay in his shop, pretending to be strict and sending me home at the end of my visit.

I ran through the ankle-deep snow. Then I turned round, and when I saw through the veil of snowflakes that Marcus was no longer watching to check that I'd turned into Schikanedergasse as he'd told me, I kept going straight on towards the Naschmarkt market.

They said on this morning's news that snow fell in Ulcinj in the middle of summer, and now people will probably ask themselves why. Why, indeed, does snow fall? In the childhood stories I'm telling you it falls to bring peace and joy. I don't think my story is different to that of most other people: childhood is a widespread phenomenon. And childhood's most pleasant moments are often concentrated in blissful, snow-covered winter days.

James Joyce, for example, has snow fall so as to set the final scene of one of the most touching stories in the history of

28

literature, which, although not as long as the history of snow, is similar to snow in that it reveals the footprints of those who've trodden this world. The ending of 'The Dead', where Gabriel Conroy realises that his wife will spend the rest of her days at his side but that the greatest event of her life was in the past, when a young man died because of his love for her, and Gabriel comprehends that everything he can give her in life is worthless compared to what the dead Michael Furey has already done for her . . . Oh, perhaps I take it all too personally. I have a soft spot for sad love stories.

Now you know why the snow falls for me. The world shines differently beneath the snow – that light falls from the sky, covering us, all we can see, and everything our senses perceive. However many times we've seen snow, the spectacle is always as fascinating as the first time. You can consider snow to be just congealed water, of course, but being rational is only good up to a point, beyond which reason destroys all joy in life. Things like snow have to stay unexplained, and therefore pure, so we can enjoy them. To stand beneath the sky as it sprinkles us with snow and reflect on the atmospheric processes which formed it is not irrational but is certainly a sorry state deserving of sympathy. For such a person, snow is just a nuisance – one of many which await them before death, the greatest unpleasantry lurking at the end.

I remember *one snowfall* better than all the others. It was during the war years, though I don't remember exactly because they've all merged into a continuum of nausea and I can't distinguish them any more. I didn't experience those years then and there, but I did spend them with you as I sifted through newspapers and books, remembering every cutting and every Web link to do with the time and place where you were living. Human nature is hopelessly corrupt and this corruption is to be found in every system which people establish. So it is with the market, so it is with the Church, so it is here, too, where I'm confined *for my own good*. It's fortunate that there's corruption, I must add, because how else would I manage to get a computer into my room if no one was bribable, and how else would I get hold of the books I need so as to be with you as often as I can?

Yes, snow was falling that winter. There was a power failure. It lasted for days, so I walked with you every night through empty Ulcinj. The ice cracked beneath our feet as we talked about all that needed to be done, about how wise and careful we needed to be to survive one more year. That's how a person cracks too, you told me: they stand firm and look as if they're going to outlast eternity. But then just a little brush with misfortune, one hardship on top of that, and one more which treads on them and they shatter like shop windows on city squares under bombardment.

The north wind blew away the clouds over Ulcinj and the cold descended on the landscape to preserve it, like the canvases of the Old Masters are conserved. The radiance of the stars reflected on the snow-covered ground. Now, when the sub-stations had burnt out and the power lines were down, when people lit their houses with candles and there were no street lights, the town shone brighter than ever before. Radiant it was, like cities beyond the memory of the living, from times which no one now remembers. We know these things only from books printed on paper *as white as snow*, paper which awaits the moment when *snow falls on the margins* and

30

it shall finally be revealed to us *why* snow falls: so that we see the word impressed on paper more clearly and also read the word – the text from which everything began.

Chapter Three

which describes human resourcefulness and falling cows, while a butcher tells us his tale of cold and loss

The line of cars was finally starting to move. I drove past the market and the suburb of Nova Mahala before heading down the narrow streets towards the Port. The thousands of people who'd been packed together like sardines on the beach that June day were now fleeing in panic. Every few seconds, one of them would bash into the side of the car. A few moments earlier they'd been putting on sun lotion to get a better tan, and now they left greasy pawprints on the windscreen when they tumbled over the bonnet. I stopped and looked down at the beach. I saw a family encamped under an umbrella: a man, a woman and three small children. Tourists from Kosovo have the custom of taking woollen blankets to the beach. The older members of their thirty-head immediate families lie on them all day, smoking and drinking *çaj rusit*, their heavily stewed black tea, which they sip out of small glass cups like a designer hybrid between a schnapps glass and a Turkish coffee cup. Now the blankets and the hot tea will come in handy. How could I not have noticed before: they have a panoply of beach/mountain gear good for both summer and winter outings. This pile of things in their PVC bag means they're equipped for all climatic conditions, from −50 to +50 degrees. The family under the umbrella sat huddled in the blankets and stared towards the left-hand end of the beach. In the wind-shadow of the headland where Hotel Jadran used to stand, a group of beachgoers were splashing around and playing volleyball in the shallows. They can only have been Russians.

I stepped on the gas a bit and drove round to Hotel Galeb, which was demolished a decade ago. The town council promised to build a new luxury hotel complex in its place, but today there are only eerie ruins with no function except perhaps a sentimental one: to remind the small Jewish community, which has settled not far from here and bought houses from the old-timers, of all its demolished temples and houses in their original homeland over the sea.

I continued on and came to the monument to the fallen fighters of the Second World War. This memorial, located just above Mala Plaža, the cove and the Old Town, hovers with outstretched wings like an oversized dove of peace and victim of radiation. Although a white dove, it doesn't seem peace-loving: it strikes me as an animal trained to carry bombs instead of letters, as if the sculptor's chisel caught the very moment when it was preparing for indiscriminate bombing. The monument has been decaying for decades, but the town councillors don't dare to have it demolished and sell the site to one of the local tycoons. If they did, they know they'd be shot by one of the former Partisans, who might need a walking stick to get around but still have a sharp eye and a steady hand.

I needed all of half an hour to get through the throng and

make it home from the monument – a drive of one or two minutes under *normal* circumstances, without people running about in the snow in their swimming trunks and flinging themselves in front of the car. But the last and biggest obstacle of the day was still ahead of me.

At the last bend before my modest home, a cow was lying on the road. I got out of the car, lit a cigarette and went up to my neighbour who was standing beside the animal and scratching his head. I asked what had happened and he replied with a candid, if somewhat rambling description of the events which had led up to one third of his assets lying here on the carriageway. Of all that he wanted to explain, the only important thing was made clear to me by his pointing finger: the concrete wall on the right-hand side of the road. I knew all the rest. A good four metres high, the wall was built to prevent rockslides from hitting the road. As far as I know, there are only two species on the planet capable of climbing near-vertical slopes: the Himalayan chamois and its predator, the snow leopard. Now the neighbour's cow had tried to graze on that near-vertical hill. It was driven by hunger because people in our region keep hundreds of cows which they don't feed. Every morning they let them out of their sheds, and herds of the stressed animals – the nightmare of every respectable Indian – roam the town until dark, feeding on the sparse grass in the parks and scavenging among the garbage which farmers leave at the market when they close their stalls. The cows are thus forced to climb over stone verges, like goats, and to use the roads, like people. The eternally hungry bovines have already browsed off all the fig bushes, grape vines and gardens in the neighbourhood. The only grass within several kilometres grows up on the hill above the retaining wall. Where many cows do not venture, one will boldly go. And that cow fell. The poor animal tried to land on its legs but the bones broke from the impact and were jutting out of open fractures on its legs. A bloody trail led from the place of the fall to where it now lay at the end of its tether, with no more strength to move.

In the meantime the neighbour's family went in action. They hopped around the cow like Lilliputians around Gulliver. His mother carted up a wheelbarrow, his youngest daughter brought a set of rusty knives and the eldest arrived with an axe in tow. Finally his son appeared, brandishing a chainsaw and full of enthusiasm about the impending massacre. When you live alongside other people you get used to all sorts of things, but slaughtering an animal in the middle of a main road still seemed a bit extreme even by our standards.

'What else can I do?' the neighbour whined in his defence. 'She's too heavy to move, and I can't just leave her here for the dogs. We'll have to cut her up, take the pieces back in the wheelbarrow and put them in the freezer, there's no other way. The butcher will be here any minute. I called him because this cow was my favourite – I can't kill her myself. I'm afraid, and my hand will tremble,' he said.

'I know this is a difficult time for you, but I won't stay. Don't take it amiss. I haven't had a proper drink yet today,' I apologised.

I glanced in the rear-view mirror as I was driving away and saw the lumbering figure of Salvatore, the butcher, arriving with his slow gait at the place of execution.

When I finally made it home, I hastily knocked back the

double Cardhu I'd decided to treat myself to. I threw myself into the armchair and turned on the television. Snow in Ulcinj in summer hadn't made the headlines because it was hindered by other, even greater wonders of nature. CNN reported a rain of frogs which had blighted Japan. The reporter was standing under a fly tent next to some Japanese who were calmly eating sushi. He tried to interview them, but they didn't share his fascination with the event. *I hope the frogs stop falling soon – my lunch break ends in ten minutes,* one of them muttered between two mouthfuls. It sure is hard to fascinate the Japanese, I thought. Even if Godzilla emerged from the ocean dressed in a white shirt, black miniskirt and little white socks like a schoolgirl, with its eyes bound with pink lace knickers, Nipponese passers-by would hardly bat an eyelid.

The news then took me to America, where people still appreciate a good miracle. A devastating earthquake had hit Los Angeles. Footage from a helicopter showed a bridge broken in half. Desperate people were clinging to a twisted steel framework and paramedics were trying to pull them up. Just as it looked as if the valiant rescuers would succeed, the ground shook again. A red pick-up rolled backwards, hitting another car. And, seconds later, dozens of vehicles came crashing down on the paramedics and their desperate rescuees like an avalanche of metal.

'Los Angeles is in flames and people are trying to flee the city in panic,' the anchorman said.

A new report followed with another human drama. A residential building was ablaze and firefighters were trying in vain to climb up to a group of occupants who'd sought refuge on the roof. Rescuers on the ground held a safety net and called out to the desperate people to jump. They threw themselves off, one after another, and were caught down below by evidently well-trained Californian firefighters. But an old lady refused to jump. Although the CNN cameraman was filming from his shoulder while running through the crowd of onlookers, I could make out in the unsteady footage that the lady was holding a tiny dog in her arms. In the end she finally jumped, but fear had a hand in things – she came down hard on the lawn, a good five yards from the safety net. The camera zoomed in on her crushed body. A Scottish terrier slipped from her arms, which would never move again. One of the firefighters triumphantly held aloft the little dog, like a shaggy trophy. 'It's alive!' he shouted. The bystanders clapped, and the camera closed in on the bewildered animal licking its paw.

Fox News showed images from New York. Manhattan woke up to find itself under water: experts couldn't yet explain why, but the sea level had risen dramatically. Whereas the CNN reporters focused on the despair which the abrupt and violent acts of nature had driven people to, the right-wingers on Fox News emphasised the optimism of their born-again viewers. The preacher in a megachurch in Texas announced euphorically: 'We told them and they didn't believe us, but now the End has finally come, rejoice, O Christians!' and behind him a gospel choir of fat black ladies blared *Jesus is coming, hallelujah!* In a student dorm in Iowa, two boys from respectable Wasp families sang *It's the end of the world as we know it and I feel fine* accompanied on acoustic guitar by a stoned, raven-haired Tanita Tikaram lookalike.

MTV reacted promptly and to the point: Strummer roared *London is drowning and I live by the river*, while an autocue at the bottom of the screen advertised the upcoming *MTV Apocalypse Awards*.

A stuffy Euronews correspondent reported from a mountain peak in Switzerland on avalanches which had buried villages in the valleys. I also learned from him that Holland had been struck by a tsunami. The information coming in spoke of hundreds of thousands of dead. Their correspondent in Russia reported about a doomsday sect, breakaways from the Orthodox Church, who saw the dreadful cruelty of nature as a sign of the Second Coming of Christ. Emaciated-looking Ivans and Natashas with colourful headscarves, who were obviously doing their best to look like matryoshka dolls, were hurrying to hide underground. Their reading of the Bible seemed to be that only those who buried themselves alive would survive the end of the world. Be it because of the rush or out of laziness, these God-fearing folk didn't dig their own holes but hid in one which turned out to have been excavated by Gazprom as part of a new gas pipeline. When the believers refused to leave the company's land, the Russian president sent in the army, who mowed them down and threw them into another pit which wasn't Gazprom's. The reporter openly voiced his revulsion at this inhumane act of the Russian authorities, but it seemed to me that the believers had achieved a significant symbolic and practical victory. They were under the ground, so they'd got what they wanted.

I turned off the television because there was a knock at the door. It was Salvatore.

'Please forgive me for coming unannounced like this, I

know you don't like visitors,' he said and extended me his right hand; in his left he was holding a butcher's knife. 'Your neighbours are waiting for me down at the cow. I told them I needed some knives from your place and would be straight back. I know we've never had much to do with each other – we've hardly ever spoken. But I hope you'll understand: I just need a little of your time.'

Salvatore had the stature of a serial killer from a horror film but the manners of an academic. I invited him in because I have a soft spot for politeness, which is a rare virtue in this mountainous and uncultured country. I noticed out of the corner of my eye that I'd left the gate to the property open in the rush to get to my drink. One careless moment and people invade your world, I thought: and not just anyone, but people in bloodstained butcher's aprons!

'Life is harsh,' Salvatore said when I'd poured him a drink and sat him down on the couch. He'd never been shown mercy, nor did he expect any. Whoever counted on mercy came to a bad end – he'd seen it many times. Today he sat and drank with me. There was no respite. Whatever happened, life always had to go on. One month earlier he'd suffered a great tragedy, one which would've destroyed most other people. But even as a boy he'd learned to live with loss: to mourn for a moment, and then soldier on. The dead can bury the dead, right? And before long he was back at work. If people don't have work they delve around in their past until life caves in on them. But he wasn't one to philosophise, he said.

He wanted to tell me about his tragedy. He arrived at the shopping centre in Bar at six o'clock each morning. The parking lot was empty. For years he'd been the first to arrive at work, although he had to drive there. He got out and leaned against the car, lit a cigarette and looked up at the bluish slopes of the Rumija mountain range. After years of looking, one glance sufficed to tell him what time of year it was.

He liked to watch the slopes burning in the summer light. The midsummer glare is merciless. It's different in September, when the days are shorter and morning comes later. Then the light is velvet, as if everything is shrouded in haze. In September the world looks like the old pictures which they write about from time to time in the paper. The people in those pictures are usually naked and have a sleepy look. He thought he looked like that too when he examined his face in the rear-view mirror of the red Zastava, he told me.

Salvatore's eyes were bloodshot and dull. He watched films until late at night and also drank, but only a little more than moderation, he emphasised. A man had to have an outlet sometimes. His wife and children were asleep when he returned from work; he didn't disturb them. He wasn't one of those men who got drunk and maltreated their family, he said. He sat in front of the television and thought about things. Different things. He had a few beers. It'd been like this for fifteen years since he'd been working at the shopping centre. At first he only worked one shift. But then their second son came along, the eldest started school and life became ever more expensive. He began working weekends, but that didn't bring in enough extra income. Then he agreed with his boss that he work two shifts: from seven in the morning till ten in the evening, seven days a week. His children lived like all the others: modestly but without want. He knew his life wasn't like that of other people, but that was the price he had to pay so his children could have a normal life. That's just the way things were. His father, too, had slaved away from dawn till dusk to raise him. People struggle and then die. That's just the way things are, he said.

He never rang when he came home. He made sure the door and the lock were well greased so they wouldn't squeak when he opened them, sneaked into the hall and locked them again. He turned the television down low so only he could hear it. When he went to the fridge or to the bathroom, too, he was careful not to wake the family. Over the years he learned to go without being heard. He even managed to get into bed without waking his wife. When he went to work in the morning, they were still sleeping. He opened the door of the children's room a little and looked at his sons. Dragan was already thirteen and resembled him. Mirko was still small. Children at that age look like their mother.

'When I drive to Bar, I imagine their alarm clocks ringing,' Salvatore said. He pictured Dragan, half-awake, stumbling towards the bathroom. After him Mirko came running, complaining that he needed to go urgently. Mirna, his wife, was already in the kitchen frying eggs. She'd contracted chronic arthritis as a young woman and every movement caused her pain. But she had a normal life with a husband and children. Like every other woman.

'When we got married I told her: "As long as I'm alive I'll make sure you can enjoy a normal life. You'll be able to live like all other women,"' he said. He imagined them eating, going to the fridge and taking out the jam and milk he'd bought the night before on the way back from work. Breakfast was over; now the boys got dressed and ready to leave for school. Before they left the house, Mirna gave them a euro each. 'This is from your Dad,' she'd say, and they'd run off cheerfully down the street. 'I see all that while I'm driving,' he said.

He'd smoke a second cigarette. In the distance he heard a Lada and knew it was the cleaning lady being brought to work by her husband. Like every morning, they'd say a polite hello and she'd unlock the front entrance. Then he'd go to the cold room and she to the cleaning storeroom, and they wouldn't meet again until the next morning.

As he prepared the meat for the day he heard the other shopping-centre staff arriving, through the cold-room door: Mirjana from the fruit and vegetable section, who was now engaged and spent the days making plans for her marriage; Zoran from the purchasing department, whose wife had been diagnosed with cancer and who wandered from doctor to doctor, getting deeper and deeper into debt, searching in vain for a cure; Branka from the health and cosmetics section, who had problems with her alcoholic father; and Aida from the bakery, who had a mute child.

He also heard the voices of the regular customers. For example, there was a lady who they knew by her first name, Stela, whose son had moved to Canada. He married a black woman there. Stela objected, but he didn't listen. Even as a child he'd been obstinate, she said. She begged him not to get hitched to that woman. Now he was punishing his mother by not getting in touch for years. Every morning Stela would buy her two croissants and then rush home: 'I have to get back – just imagine if he rings while I'm out!' she fretted day in, day out.

Although Salvatore spent most of the day in the cold room, he knew everything about those people. It was as if he listened to a radio programme about their lives all day. They chatted, argued, bitched and rejoiced about things, and he listened to it all just as if he was out there with them. At first it'd been hard to get used to the chill and isolation of the cold room, but over time he realised that it didn't matter. When he heard how hard other people's lives were and how they struggled, he was ashamed that he'd complained about his life so much.

Every morning, first thing, he sharpened the knives. He took his time and did it meticulously. 'You can see yourself in my knives like a mirror,' he said. He couldn't stand blunt knives. The blade had to pass through the meat without resistance. The cut had to be straight and clean. He was horrified when people mangled meat instead of cutting it. Some almost seemed to hate the meat they cut. It was as if they let out all their frustration on the pieces of veal and pork they got their hands on. One look at the cuts a butcher made would tell him what sort of person he was. An angry, resentful person was easiest to recognise. Butchers like that always made more cuts than necessary. They cut and realised it was wrong. Then, in their rage, they cut wrongly again. They ended up rending the meat like a wild animal. He'd seen butchers like that: if their wife had offended them or their children didn't respect them, they stabbed the meat and tore at it. There were ones who bellowed as they cleaved the meat. Some made a real mess in the butcher's shop: they dragged the pieces of meat across the floor, stamping on them and kicking them. But not him: he left all his problems at the cold-room door.

When he finished work, he left everything spic and span. It was as clean as in a hospital, he said.

Until noon, when he had his first break, he made sausages with lots of garlic; then he prepared burgers and three sorts of meat patties. Next he marinated meat in oil, salt, pepper and *herbes de Provence* – but not paprika because it would dominate the taste. He filleted pork, cut beef for soup-making, and set aside prime-quality fillets and rump steak. It was like that in the summertime: however much you prepared, the café owners bought it all.

He would take a bottle of beer out of the fridge and sit down on the bench behind the butcher's shop in the shade. He smoked two cigarettes and watched the cows and sheep tottering about the meadow, torpid from the heat. Mirjana would come and sit next to him. She would bum a cigarette like she did every day.

'What are you up to?' she asked one day.

'Watching the animals. I could watch them for hours. I grew up with animals: we had cows, sheep and goats at home,' he told her.

'I don't like animals – they scare me,' she said. 'When my husband and I have kids and they're a few years old, maybe I'll get them a dog. I've read that dogs are good for kids. Children who grow up with dogs become better people because a dog has the traits of a good person. The dog brings them up to be good, in a way. A dog is OK, but I'd never let a cat into the house. I'll invite you to my wedding. Will you come – you and your family?' she asked. Then she threw away the butt and returned to work without waiting for a reply.

He glanced at his watch: twenty past twelve. He had time

for one more cigarette. He stared at the cows which were now lying in the meadow. They didn't move or give any signs of life. He was musing on how they looked almost like rocks, when he was roused from his reflections by a voice calling his name. Turning, he saw two police officers standing beside him. Come with us, was all they said.

When they were driving in the police car he tried to find out where they were taking him, and why. The men in uniform said they were under orders not to tell him any details. The car pulled up in front of the mortuary. 'Even then I didn't know, even then I didn't think,' he said. Only when he'd set foot inside the mortuary did he notice that he still had his apron on. He'd been working all morning and the apron was blood-smeared, as was the cap which he kept on all day in the cold room. *They'll think I'm a psychopath,* he thought. He was relieved when he saw the mortuary was empty and no one could be intimidated by his appearance. At the end of the corridor he saw Mirna. She ran towards him, all in tears, and threw herself into his arms. 'Dragan's dead,' she howled, 'someone's killed our son,' she screamed and dug her fingernails into her cheeks. The blood mixed with her tears and she smeared it over her eyes and hair in her anguish.

Then the doctor appeared. He also had a bloodstained white apron and a cap. The only difference between them was the gloves the doctor wore, Salvatore said. The doctor instructed the police officers. One took Mirna to the toilet so she could wash and calm down, the other accompanied Salvatore and the doctor to the autopsy room. On a metal table in the middle, illuminated by a neon lamp, lay his son.

'Twenty-nine stab wounds, probably made with a knife,

and three slash wounds: two short ones on the chest and a long one which tore his stomach,' the doctor explained.

'It was a blunt blade – an ordinary kitchen knife like you can buy at any market,' Salvatore told him.

'How do you know?' the doctor asked.

'You can see I'm a butcher,' Salvatore said.

He asked the doctor and the policeman to leave him alone with his son.

Through the door of the autopsy room he heard Mirna crying and the voice of the policeman trying to console her.

'I know how you must feel: I also lost a child. But you have to calm down. If I'm not mistaken, you have another boy? You have to settle down and keep going for his sake,' he said. Their voices receded – they'd probably gone outside for some fresh air.

He sat down on the bench in the corner and looked around the room. It was clean and everything was in its place. The sharp implements were neatly arranged on a long table. The panes of glass in the door were immaculate, without the fingermarks which are always a tell-tale sign of negligence. The floor tiles had been polished. The only stain on them was a little puddle of blood from his son's right arm, which hung down from the autopsy table.

Salvatore got up, raised the boy's arm and laid it alongside his body, parallel to the arm on the other side. 'That was how Dragan slept: stretched out and flat on his back,' he said. He pulled up the white sheet to cover his son's body. On the shelves he found some paper towels. He wiped the blood from the floor and shone the tiles with a moistened towel. Then he sat down on the bench in the corner again.

It was cold in the room. He could see the steam of his breath. 'For a moment I thought I was back in the cold room and everything was alright. As if it was still morning and the whole day lay ahead,' he said.

Chapter Four

which tells of books and a conversation in Saint Anna's Hospital, presents the multiple murder from a different angle, and shows us Fra Dolcino fleeing the wrath of the Church and finding refuge in the Franciscan monastery on Bojana River

from: emmanuel@gmail.com
to: thebigsleep@yahoo.com

It was the article about the library fire which finally opened my eyes. The papers and Web portals were full of headlines about the killing of the Vukotić family, which is why I didn't notice it earlier. I find it unforgiveable that such a tragedy is reduced to a spectacle to be served with morning coffee. All the pain and fear of the murder victims, and all the sorrow and despair of those who survived them, is transformed into a product to increase newspaper circulation – a topic of conversation to while away the time and be utterly forgotten as soon as the front pages scream in bold about a new murder. Every day we do and say unforgiveable things, without our hand or voice trembling. We defend our right to the unforgiveable with the utmost decisiveness. Doubt and trepidation only come when fear takes over and when our lives, which we once claimed a sovereign right to and defended at whatever cost, have slipped completely from our control.

That terse report in the 'Community' column told me that the Ulcinj Library was set on fire the very same evening that the killers broke into the Vukotićs' house. As I'm sure you know, the library fire was started a few hours before the murder. Although the fire station is just twenty metres behind the library and right next to the police station, the report in the paper suggests the firefighters arrived late. They didn't set about extinguishing the fire until the damage had become irreversible and the flames had engulfed the roof of the building. By then, the book which the fire was meant to destroy lay in cinders.

The chaos in the centre of town facilitated the work of the Vukotićs' killers. I can see them now, driving towards the house along a little-used track in the dark, without headlights. They kept off the busy road to avoid detection. Although they had done an efficient job with the library, these well-organised and devoted zealots remained cautious and used the narrow dirt road leading up to the property from the back. There were no houses there, whose lights might give away those coming with evil intent – only scrub and forest between there and Cape Djerana. And forest is a good keeper of secrets.

Four men in black balaclavas opened the narrow, ground-level window and crawled through it into the cellar. The ease with which they moved and their noiseless steps showed they were adept at crime. They didn't want to wake the residents before the task was done. They quickly found the safe hidden beneath the floorboards under a thick, sumptuous carpet which, even in the dark of the house, they could be sure was Persian. One of the intruders knew the combination for opening the safe. It clicked open and he withdrew a thick book with a hard, leather binding. As he leafs through it, I can see it was

49

written by hand in a language unknown to me. The writing seems scattered, and the pages are yellowing and battered at the edges. It was as if the paper didn't absorb the ink – the letters and words are just lying on the pages, ready to flutter up and away at need.

The burglars made certain that this was the book they were looking for. But their work wasn't yet done. One of them lifted up a vase from the kitchen table and smashed it on the floor with all his might. As intended, the noise roused the residents. The woman of the household came first, running down the stairs and shouting *Who's there?!* While one of the burglars inflicted fatal wounds on her, the others ran up to the first floor, where they overpowered her husband and mercilessly killed the children. They then left the house through the front door, which they intentionally left ajar. This was meant to mislead investigators: if you hadn't witnessed the crime you'd think the woman opened the front door and let the killers into the house.

I spoke about this with Doctor Schulz today. He was particularly interested in the part of the story about the burning of books.

'Why did they burn down the library?' he wanted to know, and above all: 'Which book burned in the library? And which was stolen from the Vukotićs'?'

Dr Schulz often reminds me of my childhood: people like him are becoming steadily rarer. It's as if they belong to a different time and disappear with it. He sits patiently in his armchair beneath the large portrait of Lacan and listens to me with the greatest attentiveness. Sometimes he takes notes of what

I say. These are obviously of no real significance because all our conversations are tape-recorded, he just jots them down to add a dash of pop-psychological flavour. But he plays his role flawlessly, with no intention of adding to the interpretation – without innovations, which would destroy everything. *Rereading* is the vogue term: people produce *rereadings of rereadings* and in doing so only conceal their inability to read the text in full. Dr Schulz reminds me of Bruno Ganz and his playing of Thomas Bernhard: if you go to the Burgtheater to see *The Ignoramus and the Madman*, be it the première, the second showing, or the second season, you'll see the same actor playing the same role in the same way. Even the vanilla-scented tobacco Dr Schulz smokes in his pipe is always the same.

'I wonder what could be written in the book you're talking about?' he said. The question was rhetorical, of course, but it served well as an introduction to what was to come.

'So you're studying the case of a burned book – I must admit I also find this a fascinating topic,' he began his most instructive and interesting discourse. 'My fascination goes back to an event during my studies. Its elusive implications have accompanied me up until this day. You are . . . how should I put it . . . our conversation here was portended that day, so many years ago.

'The event I'm taking about occurred in 1977. I came here to St Anna's towards the end of that year to attend a seminar given by Lacan. Even back then I found its title threatening: *The Time of Conclusions*. One morning we gathered in the amphitheatre; we were all young and full of faith in ourselves and our mission. We listened with bated breath as he, brilliant

51

as ever, outlined the seminar he was going to hold. "Now I'd like to hear your questions," he said after his introduction.

'You may not have noticed, and maybe it's imperceptible today, but my greatest failing is vanity,' Dr Schulz told me. 'When we're young, our vanity is simply ludicrous, but no less dangerous. If you'd known me back then, you could have been sure that I'd be the one to ask the first question. And not any old question: it had to be one which told the teacher that this pupil had mastered his lessons. It was intended as a kind of declaration of loyalty: this pupil wanted to tell the teacher that he'd remain true to his teachings although he knew their weak points.

'"What is your greatest desire: to bequeath your work to the world?" I asked him.

'You haven't understood anything. On the contrary, before I die I want to completely destroy my work,' Lacan stated, and he meant it. This wasn't a threat or a vow, and even less a confession, but a cold conclusion. Back then we didn't believe our teacher would destroy every hope that we could help humanity and destroy our last illusion about the practical value of the discipline we'd devoted ourselves to.

'Why did our teacher want to destroy his work? Attempting to understand this led me on to the question: Why does an author destroy his book? Did you know that Kafka wanted to have almost his entire work destroyed? He entrusted the task to two friends. One, a woman, complied with his wish, while the other, a man, betrayed his friend's trust. It's the latter, Max Brod, who we have to thank for having Kafka's writing today.

'Destroying a book is the culmination of the drama of fatherhood,' Dr Schulz said, getting up from his armchair beneath the portrait of Lacan. 'And of the drama of *sonship*, if you like,' he added. He looked out the window and continued speaking, which created the strange impression of him talking to me and ignoring me at the same time. 'A son who burns a book is staging a revolution against the Father and his Law conveyed in that book. But a Father who burns his work deprives the son of his name and his Law. A burned book is the spot where the bond between father and son is severed.

'In *Totem and Taboo*, Freud goes back to the primal horde, only to find the tyranny of the father there too. The primal father imposes tight restrictions on his sons and punishes them harshly for any disobedience. The sons desire freedom and therefore band together to kill and eat their despotic father. Here we have the first of many revolutions, which will all run according to the same Oedipal scenario. But, as usual, remorse comes instead of freedom and leads the sons to resurrect their father's ban. All this is accompanied by the posthumous veneration of the father. Here, of course, we note the root of religion,' Dr Schulz said.

'Oh, if only it were so simple that a murder, even the murder of the father, could resolve things . . . The catch is that neither the actual death of the father nor the proclamation "God is dead" really brings liberation. The Law remains when the Father is gone. Since freedom can't be attained by patricide, one tries to achieve it by destroying the Law – the book which civilisation and culture are based on. To burn a book means to kill one's father, as poignantly described by Gérard Haddad, whom I met back at the seminar. But even if the father is killed twice, he still returns.' Then Dr Schulz suddenly turned towards me: 'As far as I can tell from the brief description you've given, those book-burners of yours must belong to a millenarian movement. The history of those movements is the history of book-burning and contempt for the Law.'

After those words, Dr Schulz paced the room in circles several times and then stopped at the bookshelf. He took out a book and laid it on the table, then sat back in his armchair. I memorised the title: *The Pursuit of the Millennium* by Norman Cohn. When he was sure I'd registered it, he added: 'But, like I say, I was more interested in the figure of the father who deprives the son of himself – the father who feels revulsion towards fatherhood.'

That same evening I asked my corrupt fallen angels, the paramedics, to get Cohn's book for me. I had it the very next day, hidden under my bed. The book would turn out to be irrefutable proof of the 'butterfly effect': a work written by a British academic, which an unconventional Central European psychiatrist discreetly showed his Vienna patient in a solitary clinic in the Alps, would lead to the solving of a murder mystery in a town on the Adriatic.

Everything is interrelated, I say to myself, repeating that worn-out phrase. The signs are a sure guide, but it's so damn hard to read them correctly and even just recognise them . . . Given the preoccupation or even obsession with health which I grew up in, I ask myself today if I couldn't and shouldn't have recognised the sign that everything would end in illness? You see, if *maman et papa* were dedicated to something, it was so-called physical health. They therefore perceived my asthenia as a punishment of God, while my corpulence, which they fought against in vain, must have seemed a heavy blow of

Providence indeed. Every morning *papa* washed himself in ice-cold water. That superfluous and painful ritual had been part of family tradition ever since his grandfather, an officer in the Austro-Hungarian army, had served in Sarajevo. He washed that way for the first time and realised that the absence of civilisation, which in his case began and ended with the absence of warm water, certainly toughened a man. Mother's morning toilet, on the other hand, lasted longer than it took to create some twentieth-century artworks. Jackson Pollock could have finished a painting in the time it took *maman* to do 'all that was necessary for a lady to be ready to leave the house', as she put it. This would be followed by a slow breakfast – cereal, yoghurt, fruit – and a schedule of morning gymnastics designed to keep her eternally healthy and young. My priorities were different: chocolate cake, for example. It and everything else I truly desired only became attainable in my parents' absence.

Hedvige had a good heart and, equally important for this anecdote, a good appetite. No sooner would *maman et papa* leave the house and I sadly blink my little eyes, than Hedvige would whiz down to the neighbourhood baker's to get some pastries, which we proceeded to devour in the pantry. We chose that secluded spot for our secret little ritual as if to highlight the gravity of our transgression. And that just whetted our appetite.

Hedvige was with me for days on end. She'd practically only leave the house when she went out on errands or was called to the school which her daughter, Marushka, attended.

The time I had to spend alone was particularly hard for me. I'd stand by the window, with black thoughts populating my little head. Everything that entered my mind spoke of the End and of irretrievable loss. Schikanedergasse would suddenly turn into a street being swallowed up by a swamp: I saw a flood of water coming and pushing in through the doors of the houses. Reeds started to grow among the parked cars and bent in a black wind bearing fallen leaves. Huge brown leaves rotted while still in the air and fell to the ground like dust. It was as if the whole world had turned into a grave, with the undertaker shovelling earth into it. *We'll be buried alive,* I thought as my heart slowed its beat, *we'll perish beneath the water and dust with nothing to show that we ever existed.*

I was obsessed at that time by an article I read in the paper about a rifle which had passed from hand to hand and circulated through the Balkans for almost a century. It so happened that every owner of the rifle was shot and killed – but not before he himself had killed someone with the accursed gun. Belgrade historians made a list of the various owners of the rifle and also those killed by it. They then fed all the available genealogical data into the computer. It turned out there was a certain order to all the killing which had at first looked so random and indiscriminate. For example, a grandson of the rifle's first owner was killed by his grandfather's weapon. The great-grandson of his killer shot a man from Herzegovina with the same rifle. The dead man's son later took possession of it and, without knowing that he was using the rifle which had killed his father, shot a certain Perović from Nikšić, who was a descendant of the rifle's first victim. When the Belgrade historians joining the dots on the rifle's huge, ramified family tree designating those who killed with it and those who were killed by it, they ended up with an outline of a butterfly with spread wings.

I concluded back then that everything I do, and everything I think, can have terrible consequences for people I don't even know. A sequence of events unfolds, unforeseeable for me but entirely logical in itself, which can forever change the lives of people, even those who'll come after me. For the first time, I clearly formulated the idea which has possessed me up until today: if I could comprehend the pattern by which the actions of people in one place and time impact on the lives of people in another, I'd be able to understand how the world works. I'd be in possession of the matrix which governs the unfolding of history. Then I'd be able to make sure that none of my actions caused sorrow or pain to others.

After that, *maman et papa* would enter my mind. I'd see their car racing along a winding forest road at night. The car's headlights would illuminate the huge trees which stood by the roadside like grim sentinels lining the travellers' way to a secret and sinister destination. Another time I'd see them crossing an intersection, with a busload of schoolchildren inexorably speeding towards them from the side. Or I'd see their car breaking through the crash barrier and plunging over a cliff into the sea, which beat and foamed against sharp rocks far below. The ending was always the same and had them dying in the crushed body of the car.

Those visions were so real, so convincing, that I'd instantly be overcome by a fear that they really were dead. No one could dispel my fear, not even Hedvige when she returned to the apartment. She'd come running up to me: 'Master Emmanuel, it was all just a dream!' she'd say. I'd spend the rest of the day glued to the window in fear and trembling incessantly. I'd stare down the street and wait for the only thing which could bring relief: my parents' return. But fear wasn't the worst. Along with it there came a paralysing guilt. The feeling that I was to blame for their death was all-powerful and pervasive, and inseparable from the fear. I think you could say that I feared my thoughts and acts had evoked their death. An unbearable weight pressed down on my young shoulders like a boulder determined to crush me: not their death itself but the thought that they'd only died because of me.

By the time they finally returned I'd be a trembling heap on the floor. They'd reprimand Hedvige, who each time, rightfully, perceived that as the worst injustice and withdrew downcast into the kitchen. I'd be taken to my room and put to bed, as usually happened when they didn't know what to do with me. Through the bedroom door I'd hear my mother crying. The realisation that she was miserable because of me dealt yet another blow to my tormented body.

Later, when the voices in the apartment died down and the streetlights were on outside, Hedvige would slink into my room, sit at my feet and read me stories from her hidden book. 'As we agreed, no one is to hear a word about this,' she'd whisper and put her fat finger to her lips. That was another of our rituals: she'd take the book from her apron, wink to me – her accomplice – mutter 'Now, where did we stop last time?' and start reading me the latest adventures of the Son of God, who asked *Father, father, why have you forsaken me*? as he suffered to save us all, me included.

Dr Schulz knows the things I've told you about myself. He knows a lot. But there's one thing he doesn't know, the most important thing, and I'm going to tell it only to you because it's the key for you to unlock the secret of the Vukotić murders:

there's a *third book* – one which its author called *The Book of the Coming*. It is the reason for all this happening.

For you to understand, we have to go far back into the past.

I first found out about the author while reading Marcel Schwob's *Imaginary Lives*. And as these things usually go, I discovered that book coincidentally and indirectly via Borges, who turned out to have read Schwob before he was even twenty and went on to virtually become his pupil.

One of the twenty-two literary portraits Schwob wrote is the story of the heretic Dolcino. The historical Fra Dolcino was born around 1250, we can assume. We have to be more careful when trying to determine his place of birth: most researchers consider that he *might* have been born in Novara. Schwob's Fra Dolcino pursued his sacred studies at the church of Orto San Michele, 'where his mother raised him so he'd be able to touch the beautiful wax figurines with his little hands'. The boy grew up with the Franciscans, and the friar who instructed him claimed he was accepted into the order by Saint Francis himself. I see myself standing beside the sweet boy as he learns to speak with the birds, which aren't afraid of him and often come to land on his shoulders. The boy snaps out of his daydreaming and remembers he has to go to the monastery, where Schwob says he 'sang in a sonorous voice with the brethren'. Barefoot, he rushes like a whirlwind through the crowded lanes and markets.

The boy lived from begging and found great enjoyment in mendicant ways. Schwob describes how, one summer day, the townsfolk were cruel to the boy and his brethren. Hungry

59

and thirsty, they took refuge from the heat with their empty baskets in an unfamiliar courtyard. Here the boy experienced a miracle – the first of many great miracles which years later would lead him to believe he was *the chosen one*. A curtain of grapevine formed before his eyes, and leopards and other wild animals from faraway lands frolicked behind it. Young women and men in bright raiment played violas and lutes. When the boy lowered his gaze to his basket, it was full of fragrant loaves of bread, reminiscent of the time Jesus fed the five thousand with five loaves and two fish.

Fra Dolcino's biographers note that Dolcino was falsely accused of theft – in Vercelli, by all accounts. Although innocent, he was tortured. Humiliated by his mistreatment, he fled to the city of Trento, where he came across a sect whose name sounded so pure: the Apostolics. Later, in 1300, he was to don the white robe and become leader of the Apostolic movement. Now Dolcino was indoctrinated with the esoteric teachings of Gioacchino da Fiore. Thomas Aquinas refuted Da Fiore's ideas in *Summa Theologica*. Nevertheless, Dante placed Da Fiore in Heaven. In his *Inferno*, Dante also mentions Fra Dolcino, whom Mohammed warned to prepare well for the conflict with the Novarese.

Under the influence of Da Fiore's teachings, Dolcino would turn the Apostolics into a brotherhood known as the Dolcinians. Night after night, Dolcino listened to the stories of the older brethren about Da Fiore's wisdom and kindness, and also about the history of the world, which Da Fiore divided into three ages. There by the campfire high up in the mountains, in the empty lands where neither merchants' caravans nor soldiers pass and the Apostolics were safe, a lamb appeared to

Dolcino in a dream. It came down the hill towards him with a flight of tiny red birds hovering above it.

Dolcino wakened his followers at dawn and told them the revelation which had come in his dream: there had been the age of the Old Testament, he said, when people were created to settle the land; there had been the age of our Lord Jesus Christ and his apostles with their modesty and poverty; then there had been the age of decay and disaster caused by the Church and its greed. 'But an age will come, the age I am bringing –,' he proclaimed, his eyes streaming tears and his voice trembling like a sparrow in the January frost, 'an age of modesty and poverty, when the sword of worldly power and might will no longer hang over our heads. The lamb said to me: *You are my word and my promise, I am coming with you to stay for ever.*'

Now Dolcino and his band of revolutionaries wandered the Novara area. They were joined by the poor and the ignorant, inebriated not so much by the promise of a better world to come as by the prospects of plunder. The Dolcinians, who after their teacher's 'sermon on the mount' no longer doubted they were the beloved of God, gave themselves over to forbidden bodily pleasures. Churches burned late into the night in the lands they passed through, as did the houses of any who refused to renounce the authority of the Pope and were promptly slain. Dolcino absolved the marauders, rapists and killers of their sins. The Dolcinians knelt before him, ragged and filthy, with the dried blood of yesterday's victims under their nails. 'To the pure all things are pure, but to the corrupt and unbelieving nothing is pure,' Dolcino recited the words of Paul the Apostle. And no sooner had his followers crossed themselves than they were ready for new misdeeds.

A certain Father Tomaso hung from an oak in front of one of the many churches the Dolcinians committed to the flames. When he'd seen the rabble carting away the pewter, candlesticks and fabrics from his church, he turned to Dolcino and thundered: 'You call for a return to Christ, but you're blind to his works and deaf to his words! Does not our Lord say: *For many shall come in my name, saying, I am Christ; and shall deceive many . . . And many false prophets shall rise, and shall deceive many . . . Then if any man shall say unto you, Lo, here is Christ, or there; believe it not. For there shall arise false Christs, and false prophets, and shall show great signs and wonders; insomuch that, if it were possible, they shall deceive the very elect.* Are those not his words?'

Challenged to a theological duel, Dolcino decided to withdraw without loss. Instead of parrying the presumptuous priest with a sagacious response, which his followers keenly awaited, Dolcino just muttered: 'Kill him.'

The Church soon set about hunting down Dolcino with all the means and forces at its disposal. The *Statutum Ligae contra Haereticos* was passed in Scopello on 24 August 1305. This amounted to Fra Dolcino's death sentence: from that day on, his end drew rapidly nearer like a stone falling into a well.

The most interesting period in Dolcino's scarcely documented life, from the point of view of your and my story, is the time between 1300 and 1303. Fleeing the wrath of the Church, he spent these years 'somewhere in eastern Dalmatia', the sources say. But we can assume that Dolcino didn't feel safe even there, at the 'edge of the world'. I can see him now at a marketplace in the hinterland of Split and running into one of the Franciscan friars who he'd begged with as a boy. The meeting was cordial and their friendship deep. Torn between loyalty to the Church and loyalty to his old friend, the friar chose the latter. He was journeying to the Franciscan mission in Ulcinj, which had been extended into a monastery in 1288 by the kindness of Helen of Anjou. Since he was continuing on his way at dawn, he suggested to Dolcino: 'Why not come along? Your secret will be safe with me.' And Dolcino thought: Ulcinj is *terra incognita* indeed – they'll never find me in that land of dragons!

The fugitive Dolcino and his friend travelled south through Dalmatia. Several weeks later they arrived on the banks of Bojana River in the town which would be marked on Venetian etchings over a century later as *Dolcigno in Dalmatia*.

Dolcino spent his days by the river. He carved pipes from the reeds that grew there, and with their music he charmed the fish of the water and birds of the air. But Dolcino had a mission, and he couldn't build the Kingdom of God on earth while hiding in Ulcinj. The night before departing back to his home region, where he would once again head the Dolcinians by Lake Garda, he had another dream. He saw that he'd die at the stake. But that wouldn't be his end: he dreamed that he'd be resurrected. He entrusted this dream and the date of his resurrection to only one person – his good and faithful friend, the Franciscan friar. He took down Dolcino's words and locked the manuscript into a chest, which he secretly immured deep in the walls of the monastery.

One peaceful evening by Lake Garda, Dolcino met Margaret of Trento, who before dawn would become his lover. He'd led his followers all the way to Mount Rubello, there to dig in and await the final battle. One year later, the army of the

Church would come against them with all its might. A thousand of his followers would be killed, while Dolcino and Margaret would be captured and burned at the stake. Schwob writes that Dolcino 'asked just one favour of their executioners: that in the hour of their suffering they be allowed to keep on their white robes like the apostles on the lampshade in the church of Orto San Michele', where his mother had taught him faith. But he begged in vain – he was forced to watch his lover burn to death. Before his own turn came, he was castrated, blinded, and had his nose, ears and fingers cut off.

As his head blazed like a torch, Dolcino remembered the day as a boy when he was driven by hunger, thirst, heat and the absence of human clemency – and saw leopards and heard the song of happy people. Before he breathed his last, he had a vision of himself descending from the mountain bringing baskets of *pane dolce* to the people of the valley: a gift to the poor from his master, the Saviour.

Chapter Five

which tells of trust, a lie under pressure, proud pregnant women and an old liaison, and the demands of the murder victim's brother for revenge in this world or the next

Salvatore finished his story. He sat there with his elbow on his knee and fist on his chin, staring into the emptiness before him. He stayed like that in silence for a while, like Rodin's *Thinker* who'd just reached the end of all thoughts. I thought I saw tears in his eyes. But Salvatore was a tough guy. He jumped to his feet, downed his – or rather *my* – whisky, and said in a very businesslike manner: 'So that's agreed, then?'

Like everyone who approaches me, Salvatore didn't trust the police. And quite justifiably so, because even if the police found the killer, his tracks could be covered again for the right price. If the police failed to protect the felon in any way, there was always the court: the criminal could rely on its corruptibility even if the case he'd paid to cover up was taken all the way to the Supreme Court.

Salvatore therefore wanted me to find the killer.

'You're a wreck of a man: you don't *need* anything any more, you don't *want* anything any more, not even money. I can trust you,' he told me. I took that as a compliment.

'I'll think about it,' I said.

'You'll do it, I know.' He smiled and shook my hand.

Salvatore's story didn't surprise me because he'd been dogged by misfortune all his life. His first and greatest misfortune was to be born in this country. As with the majority of things which cause us lifelong suffering, he had his parents to thank. We're all victims of our parents' inability to resist the reproductive urge. We've all been at the receiving end of the fascism of nature, whose casualty count far surpasses that of any criminal regime or system we've seen – and every single one of them has been criminal. Instead of pictures of Hitler and Stalin, textbooks which teach schoolchildren about the greatest enemies of humankind should show a picture of a forest in spring.

His parents went one step further in crime against their son: they decided to raise him in this country. Salvatore's father, Simone, had been stationed in Ulcinj when fascist Italy fell. Enchanted by the natural beauty of the town, and even more by the beauty of its women – one of whom would later become his wife, this cheerful and ever primped-up stereotype Italian decided to stay on. They say he left an olfactory trail of hair grease and aftershave behind him so that when you went downtown you'd always know where he'd been that morning. He came to Ulcinj as an occupier and ended up as the object of town jokesters and the jealousy of many a husband.

Simone lived in Ulcinj more or less peacefully. What occasional bother he had was mainly of his own making – at least up until the Trieste Crisis. Then anti-Italian demonstrations were organised throughout the country. Party leaders came from Podgorica to ensure that the 'spontaneous expression of popular rage' in Ulcinj went off according to plan. One of them heard there was an Italian living in town. The people of

Ulcinj said in Simone's defence that he was good-natured – a harmless clown, whose only flaw was being a Casanova. But the Comrades from Podgorica were unyielding: Simone was Italian, therefore he was suspicious and had to be punished.

And punished he was: he had to march at the head of the demonstrations and carry the biggest *Trieste is ours* placard – him, of all people!

*

I laughed at that anecdote again as I parked in front of the house. The muezzin's call came up from town once more. I didn't have much time – this night was going to be short. I planned to read the peculiar mails again and try to find some clue in them. While reading, I'd help myself to some whisky: there's nothing wrong with a man enjoying his work.

One day you open a mail and, whoom, you find out you're a father. All your life you've refused every possibility of fatherhood – the very thought is repellent. You're doing just fine, you think. You don't have time for anything more and everyone else can just jump in the lake. Your liver is a write-off and every next bottle could kill you, if your heart doesn't get you first. They've prescribed heart tablets but you don't take them properly. You fervently hope the doctor was right when you asked: *How much longer have I got?* and he replied: *With a lifestyle like that – a few years at best.*

You'll go for sure, but not in peace (not that you deserved it, but you hoped for it all the same). And then the twist: you get a mail and suddenly you're a father. You of all people, who was overcome by despair and anger because of neighbourhood children toddling around all summer's day on the terraces of their parents' houses too close to yours, waddling about and tirelessly repeating their *ga-ga-ga*, which sufficed to evoke applause and ovations – at least from their parents – who always channelled all their interpretative potential into trying to tell who their unsightly child took after. You of all people, who was struck and horrified by the uniquely proud gait of expectant mothers, who with every step seemed to want to say: *Look, I've fulfilled my function, I've justified my existence, I'm a mother.* As if she'd written *Anna Karenina* rather than getting pregnant! As if she was going to deliver the ultimate explanation of human misfortune rather than just reproduce, as nature has done for thousands of years and will do after her, too. You of all people, who felt nausea around men who, with the help of the whole feeble-minded community, convinced themselves that their lives were meaningful when they became fathers; these were men who got married when they didn't know what to do with themselves, and when they didn't know what to do with the marriage – they had children, and later they didn't know what to do with the children; in the end they died, but only after they'd become religious and turned for help to the world's oldest breakdown assistance service: the Church. You of all people, who maintained that the most intelligent, sophisticated and sensitive people doubted, re-examined and repented: they bequeathed us art and philosophy, but not progeny. It was the others who multiplied. Creatives died in loneliness, while the others produced herds of offspring. Humankind was thus the product of the careful selection of the worst. Yes, you of all people, who said and believed these things.

When I first saw the woman who I'd eventually conceive Emmanuel with, fatherhood was the last thing on my mind. She strode into my office briskly and proudly, with an air of ceremony. Just like Dragan Vukotić came strolling in some twenty-five years later. Unlike her, he immediately offered me money: he threw an envelope full of large banknotes onto the table and delivered me a speech he'd obviously painstakingly prepared. He told me he had the means – money wasn't an issue – but he expected me not only to find out who his brother's killer was but also to catch him before the police did. I was to bring the killer to him, and he'd mete out justice himself. There was no doubt in my mind that he meant what he said. And from what I knew about this unpleasant new client, it wouldn't be the first time. One of his building sites would be the tomb for his brother's killer: he'd throw their body into the foundations and cover it with concrete, or he'd brick them into the attic of one of his buildings. He was a tireless developer, as if he hadn't already raised dozens of buildings and earned tens of millions of euros. *Why do people who have fifty million to their name work hard to earn another?* I remember thinking as I slipped the bulging envelope into the pocket of my jacket.

She didn't offer money, but she offered what I desired much more – herself. And she did so in a stylish, discreet way by telling she *had a lot to offer*. The next morning she woke up in my bed. As soon as she opened her eyes, she woke me too. 'Don't tell me you've forgotten: you have a lot of work today,' she said, and turfed me out of my own house.

I went into town, had two or three drinks at the Port and then got down to business. The case seemed simple: one of those leading to an explanation which ultimately no one is satisfied with. The explanation of the death of loved ones is usually quite banal, and for some reason people find that hard to accept. I've never had any problem with banality. For me it's always meant convenience.

Her father had disappeared and it was my job to find him. He was in love with this town and had spent his summer holidays here for thirty years already, she told me. In fact, he lived in Ulcinj for more than half the year: he arrived as early as April, when the shad fishing season begins, and went straight from the plane to Bojana River, where his fishing crew was waiting. He didn't leave until December, after the mullet season. At first she thought he might have drowned because he'd been known to go out in heavy sea with a sirocco blowing: she imagined he'd tried to return to the river but the swell capsized him in the estuary. But his boat was moored by his cabin and all the fishing gear was there. She checked his bank account: he'd withdrawn a certain amount before he disappeared, but nothing significant.

I went out on Bojana River by boat and had a talk with fishermen who'd known him. What they had to tell me was of no help: *A peaceable sort of guy, great to have as a neighbour. We were so surprised when he disappeared, who'd have thought – but there you go, these things happen.* So I puttered down to his cabin. I'd forgotten to bring the key, so I forced the door.

Inside it was like a pharmacy: spick and span and orderly. Jars stood in file like German fusiliers at inspection. The bed was made and tucked in, barracks-style. His clothes were all on coat-hangers in the wardrobe and he'd tied sprigs of lavender to them to keep away the moths. That was a first warning sign for me – I don't trust orderly people. You can only expect the worst of someone who worries about things so diligently. I decided to search the cabin.

When I found photographs of a boy in the sleeping bag under the bed, I realised where this was heading. The boy was only ten, with black hair and a face full of birthmarks. The photos showed him naked on a sandy beach – they'd obviously forced him to pose. One of the photos had a phone number on the back: it began with the calling code for Albania.

If the old pervert had gone to Albania, there was only one person who could have taken him there: Johnny. After a few years in Germany, Johnny had come back with a hoary, money-eyed Teutoness and a powerboat which was the fastest on the coast at the time. The old woman died soon afterwards and left all her money to him; Johnny soon drank and whored it away, and now all he had left from the whole German episode was the powerboat – still fast enough to smuggle goods and people to Albania.

I found him sleeping at the dock, thoroughly drunk, with his head on the table. After I'd poured a bucket of water over him and slapped him around a bit, he was ready to cooperate.

'I've chucked a case of beer and a bottle of Scotch into your boat so you know I value your labour,' I told him.

'Gimme me a cigarette and tell me what you want,' he said.

'The German who disappeared two weeks ago: what do you know?'

'Five hundred deutschmarks and I know everything.'

We met at three hundred. And it was worth every cent of it. You don't hear a story like that every day, even when you're in my line of work. As I'd assumed, Johnny had taken the paedophile to Albania. Pimps were waiting there and took them to a house by the beach, where boys were kept confined.

'You know me, I've seen lot – thank God I've got a strong stomach, but *that* made even me feel sick,' Johnny said. 'I left him there and went back to the boat. Not five minutes had passed and I'd just opened a warm beer, when there was a commotion in front of the house. Then shots rang out. A lot of shots, several magazines full, I'm pretty sure it was a Yugoslav service pistol. *Stuff the old man*, I thought, and started up the powerboat to move away from the coast a bit. Through my binoculars I saw a man with an Albanian skullcap coming out of the house, carrying a boy in his arms. Two women ran out of the undergrowth towards them. I turned the steering wheel and stepped on the gas. Fortunately the old man had paid me in advance.

I stayed there with Johnny until evening. We didn't talk. What was there to say? We just drank beer after beer and watched the river flowing by. I didn't feel like going home, where she was waiting for me, impatient to hear news of her father who she seemed to truly love.

She was a wonderful girl and didn't deserve to find out. As soon as I heard Johnny's story I decided I'd lie to her. And I did. For a month I told her: 'I'm onto something,' then 'I'm making good progress,' and finally, 'I think I'm really close now.' She became more and more vulnerable and would burst into tears ten times a day without visible reason. The whole thing had become an ordeal for her. I had to put an end to it and was just waiting for the right moment.

One morning I woke up and thought how happy I was

with her. I kissed her hair and leaned over to whisper a few affectionate words. The time had come – I broke the news to her at breakfast that her father was dead. I told her that he'd been fishing near the far arm of the Bojana River delta. He must have strayed into Albanian waters. Border guards came and hailed out to him in Albanian. He answered in German . . . They shot him. He was buried there, in Albania – the grave could be anywhere.

'I knew it,' she repeated through her tears.

'I'm sorry,' I said. 'Now you'll have to find a way to continue your life. I presume you'll be going soon: you must have a lot of commitments waiting at home.'

She looked at me as if I'd stabbed her in the back. When I returned from work that evening she was gone. She didn't leave a farewell letter, only an envelope with money and the message: *For the extra costs.*

As it turned out, she also left me a son, who'd send me mails a quarter of a century later. Now I stood at the computer printing those texts, although I knew his fantasies wouldn't help me in the investigation. Before I left the house, I checked I had everything: key, mails, revolver and bottle. I'd left my phone in the car and could hear it ringing. It was Dragan Vukotić. He wanted to know if I had any news for him.

'Not yet, but soon,' I said.

'And when might *soon* be, seeing as we won't be around tomorrow?' he snarled.

'Listen, I'm onto a hot trail and following it like a bloodhound,' I told him. 'I think it's just a matter of hours until I nail him down.'

'I hope you do, for your sake – I'll have my revenge, in this world or the next.'

The fellow's name was Lazar – I learned that from the Vukotićs' neighbours. It was incomprehensible to me how a police force, even one as ignorant and apathetic as ours, could overlook such an important detail. They probably gave up on their work, which they were never terribly motivated about anyway, and laid down their batons and pistols to sit and wait like so many others. But not me: I, with my Protestant work ethic, have always felt lonely amidst Balkan irresponsibility and laziness.

So his name was Lazar and he worked for the Vukotićs as a caretaker. The neighbours weren't able to tell me when the Vukotićs first employed him, nor where he originally came from. And they didn't know, of course, where he'd gone after killing the family which had accepted him. 'The Vukotićs led a secluded life: we didn't feel welcome there, and so we never dropped in,' they told me.

As soon as I found out about Lazar, every piece of the puzzle fell into place. The Vukotićs had opened up for him because they knew him. He robbed them because he knew the house: as caretaker he had access to every corner of every room. He'd probably discovered they had a safe while repairing the floorboards in the living room. It was presumably then that he conceived the crime he ultimately committed. Only one thing had me fazed: the safe which my son speaks about in his mails. Inspector Jovanović didn't mention a safe when I bribed him to tell me everything he knew about the case. So now I phoned him. He answered, drunk and despairing.

'Listen, mate, I think you forgot to tell me one important detail about the Vukotić murders,' I reproached him. 'Was there a safe at the house and had it been broken into?'

'Yes,' he mumbled and replaced the receiver.

Good, I said to myself: I have a suspect who had a motive. Now I just have to find the scumbag. The way things are going, I'll still manage to get tanked up tonight.

The snow seemed to be falling more thickly now. A right bloody blizzard! Even with the high beam on, I could hardly see two metres in front of me.

Lines of refugees struggled past by the roadside. When the snow first came in June, people still hoped it was a *practical joke of nature*. But then the sea rose and carried away the joke. When day dawned, the foundations of the hotels and planned skyscrapers on Velika Plaža beach, hyped up to be a copy of the bluish, futuristic towers of Abu Dhabi, were under water. A few days later the sea swamped a village of weekenders up behind the beach. Ugly, illegally built houses sank in the swirling waters as the sea took over the responsibility of the building inspectorate. Whoever fled when the first waves were lapping their houses was able to take a few belongings with them. The optimists copped it bad, as usual: they'd thought the worst-case scenario was far-fetched, so they eventually had to be evacuated by helicopter from the roofs of their houses. People struggled to the town in makeshift rafts and boats and kissed the ground when they landed, as if they'd discovered a new continent. But the water kept surging further inland until it also flooded the suburbs. Camps were organised in hilly parts of town for the people who'd *been forced to leave their homes*, as all reports in all languages said in the same pathos-ridden tone. These folk now plodded the town like zombies in search of food. The shops had long been closed because supplying a town surrounded by water was impracticable, so the impertinent starvelings forced their way into houses and tried to steal food. Contrary to all international conventions on the rights of refugees, the residents shot them and threw their bodies out onto the road so cars would run over them and hungry dogs tear them up.

They announced on the radio that there'd been another fifty-centimetre rise in the sea level *globally* – they used precisely that word. In Ulcinj itself, the water reached all the way up to the town council building. They took the opportunity to remind listeners that the Bojana River sometimes used to overflow its banks in winter months before the dam on the Drin River was built, with the floodwater coming all the way up to where the post-earthquake council building was built. The studio guest was an environmentalist, an idiot who claimed this was yet more proof of the theory that all of nature was in equilibrium.

'The water has returned to where it once was, you see, because water has a memory, just like the planet remembers,' he said with thrill in his voice.

'But what's happening now, in your view?' the compère wanted to know. 'Where is this wave of cold coming from? And these floods?'

'I don't know,' the ecologist admitted, 'but I appeal to listeners not to be taken in by stories about a catastrophe, because one thing is certain: there is a rational explanation.'

Of course, just like there's an irrational one. As usual, all we lack is an explanation which might explain things.

'And now to recap on today's main news,' the anchorman recited: *People all around the planet are awaiting the end of the world tonight.*

Then the international news editor took the microphone. Among the mass of trivia he read, a story from Izmir caught my attention. A man with a deranged son had decided to clean up an overgrown and neglected olive grove. It had once belonged to a prominent dervish who taught that the olive tree brings people closer to God.

Although he was getting on in years, the man worked day after day in the olive grove. It was close to the sea but far from the road. The only way up to the dervish's host of olive trees was along steep, narrow paths, over dry-stone walls and through thick scrub. But the man didn't mind. The more effort he invested in the task he'd set himself, the sooner God would heed his prayers and heal his son, or so he thought.

When the young man asked if he could go with him and help with cleaning up the olive grove, his father concluded that God had heard his prayers and taken pity on him. Ever since childhood, the young man had lived in the confines of his room, alone with his attacks of madness and the medication which didn't help. His father naturally interpreted the wish to join him in this good work as a first sign of his son's recovery.

They set off together for the olive grove one morning. That evening, the son returned home alone.

The police inquest revealed that he had killed his father and thrown his body into the sea.

When they asked him why he did it, he said God had ordered him to.

Chapter Six

in which Emmanuel tells of the false messiah Sabbatai Zevi, a secret society of his resolute followers, the burial of The Book of the Coming *and the day of its resurrection*

from: emmanuel@gmail.com
to: thebigsleep@yahoo.com

As I've mentioned, Fra Dolcino left a manuscript in the Franciscan monastery on the banks of Bojana River announcing he would be resurrected. It was hidden in the walls of the friary. Several years later, when it became clear that all further resistance to the furious Novarese besieging Mount Rubello was futile and only defeat and death lay ahead, he entrusted his secret to a handful of his closest pupils.

Over three centuries later, in the garden of the imperial palace in Istanbul, the Sultan asked: *Where do you wish to be exiled?* Sabbatai Zevi replied: *To Ulcinj*. He had Dolcino's secret in mind.

What we read today as the biography of Sabbatai Zevi *may* correspond to the historical truth about him. On the other hand, it may be that most of the things we know about him, starting with the year of his birth and through to the year of his death, are only what he *wanted* us to know. Sabbatai Zevi was a first-rate manipulator, a Wildean figure before Wilde, with his life as his *chef-d'oeuvre*. His antics, sometimes incomprehensible and ludicrously inconsistent but always spectacular, were part of a grandiose project intended to convince the Jews that he was the Messiah. There's not the slightest doubt that he believed it himself.

The year of Zevi's birth is given as 1626. Was that really so, or did Zevi dictate that year to his biographers so that the very date of his birth would seem to confirm his messianic status? After all, there's a Jewish belief that the Messiah will appear on the anniversary of the destruction of the Temple. Zevi's playing with dates of great significance to Jews doesn't end there: the self-proclaimed Messiah was born in Smyrna, now Izmir, on 9 August. That was a Sabbath. He died in Ulcinj on 30 September 1676. That was Yom Kippur.

Zevi died ten years after the failure of his key prophecy – the one according to which he was the King who would return the Jewish people to Israel. Zevi had presaged that this would occur in 1666. He certainly reckoned with the interesting associations awoken by the three sixes. In fact, his whole biography is in three sixes: the year of his birth, his unfulfilled prophecy and his death all end in a six.

The books say that Zevi stood out even as a child. He didn't get on easily with the other boys studying to be rabbis. He had periods of deep melancholy alternating with phases of wild euphoria. (Dr Schulz would definitely have recognised the symptoms of bipolar disorder.) At the time, many considered them a sign that the young Zevi was *the chosen one*. At the age of twenty-five, Zevi proclaimed: 'I am the Messiah and will return my people to Israel,' and he immediately declared the abolition of God's Law. He called on the followers gathered around him to eat non-kosher food. He put on a lunatic performance and publically wedded the Torah. In a later phase of his messianic madness, he tore up and trampled on the Torah, and then desecrated leather tefilins containing the holy verses. This man, whom two women had left because he'd shown no interest in them, now became sexually insatiable. He demanded of his followers that they bring him their maiden daughters to create a harem. What was more, he claimed he could have intercourse with virgins and they would remain pure.

Zevi's theologians wrote: 'As long as taboos regarding incest prevail on Earth it will be impossible to carry out union *from above.* The mystic annulment of the ban on incest will allow man to *become like his Creator and learn the secrets of the Tree of Life.*'

While Zevi enjoyed the pleasures of promiscuity, the Sultan was worried. On 6 February 1666, he ordered that Zevi be arrested. The Jewish prophet had become a danger to his throne. Jews from all over Europe poured into the Empire to follow the Messiah. Others were preparing to sell all their belongings and follow him to Israel. Many Christians, even learned ones, attentively and optimistically awaited confirmation that Zevi held the truth. Henry Oldenburg wrote to Spinoza: 'All the world here is talking of the return of the Israelites to their own country. Should the news be confirmed, it may bring about a revolution in all things.'

Instead of leading to revolution, Zevi was led in chains before the Sultan. He was given the choice: Islam or death. If he didn't wish to adopt Islam, the Sultan was prepared to let him demonstrate his power: a master archer would loose an arrow at his breast, and if he was indeed the Messiah it certainly wouldn't be difficult for him to perform a miracle and stop the arrow. Zevi didn't hesitate for an instant: he removed his Jewish cap and donned a Turkish turban. The Messiah had changed faith at the last moment.

Aziz Mehmed Efendi, as Zevi was called after his conversion to Islam, didn't relinquish Judaism completely or sincerely, and certainly not voluntarily and free of coercion. He continued to perform Jewish rites and even to preach in synagogues. The fact that he'd become a Muslim didn't prevent him from continuing to claim he was the Jewish Messiah. The Sultan, who'd hoped Zevi's conversion would make Jews flock to Islam, watched this messianic carnival with increasing consternation.

In the end, he decided to banish Zevi. It seems this is just what Zevi had been hoping for. He tried to persuade the Sultan that Ulcinj was an ideal town for exile – at the outer edge of the Empire, at the end of all roads. He'd be quite far away and out of sight there, in the fortress above the sea.

Ulcinj was populated at this time by pirates: both local buccaneers and Barbary corsairs. It was the most recalcitrant town in the whole of the Ottoman Empire. The people of Ulcinj feared neither God nor master. Being so wild and reckless, they'd sabre Zevi if he dared to bother them with his follies, the Sultan thought. 'Let it be Ulcinj then,' he pronounced.

The Ulcinj pirates were a plague on shipping and even raided the Venetian possessions in the Adriatic. In the years to come, the Sublime Porte's conflict with these outlaws would escalate into an undeclared but no less savage war. The Pasha of Skadar was ordered to attack and set fire to a dozen of the Ulcinj pirates' vessels. When the Sultan sent a missive to Ulcinj the following year demanding that further ships be burned, the pirates killed the messenger and threw his body from the town's walls.

The Venetian authorities, for their own part, were itching to take action but realised that Ulcinj lay in Turkish territory. They didn't want to risk war with the Empire. Instead, they sought to resolve the problem by diplomatic means. One Venetian dispatch even appealed to the Sultan's vanity: 'All the inhabitants of Dalmatia and Albania are astonished that you allow the pirates of Ulcinj to so audaciously flout your authority.'

The ship carrying Zevi and twenty-nine families of his followers approached Ulcinj. A black cloud was circling above the town and the travellers watched it in trepidation. As they disembarked on the beach below the fortress, the birds were on the sand, waiting with beady eyes. They seemed to be sizing up the newcomers, whose hands trembled and knees knocked: 'As if we'd arrived in Hell!' one of the women wailed. More and more of the feathered creatures poured forth, cawing, from caverns beneath the fortress, which would ultimately collapse in the earthquake of 1979, and rose up above Zevi and his following like a black flood to sow fear in even the bravest hearts. Imagine the sky above us in black turmoil as we ascend the stone stairs towards the fortress gate. Anxiety and despair are in the eyes of Zevi's followers, but in Zevi's I see only joy, for the circling murder of crows which blocks out the sun has shown him *the sign*.

Fra Dolcino's followers had been unable to keep the secret he'd entrusted to them. Drunken mouths let it slip out and inquisitive ears were listening. As stories have a way of finding those who want to hear them, the story about Fra Dolcino and his hidden manuscript made it all the way to Smyrna. Zevi listened with disdain to those who spoke of Dolcino being a madman, illusionist and trickster. He knew Dolcino had hidden his book because he intended to return. But there could only be one Messiah. Therefore Zevi was determined to destroy the book of the 'false prophet'.

Zevi spent his days in Ulcinj in writing and prayer. He carved the Star of David into the wall of his tower and there he spoke with God, whom he'd never renounced. Zevi left Ulcinj only twice: once he went to Bojana River to try and find Dolcino's book in the ruins of the Franciscan monastery; the other time he travelled to the Archdiocese in Bar to try and find some trace of the book or at least rekindle his hope that the search would bear fruit.

Zevi would have gone to the very ends of the earth to find Dolcino's book: his thoughts probed the distance in search of it. But the whole time it seems to have been right under his very nose.

Twenty years after Zevi's death, the Morean War was raging. A Venetian fleet assembled in the sea off Ulcinj. It was 10 August 1696. Historical documents state: 'The aim of the attack was to take the town and destroy the pirate nest because all attempts by the Venetians to wipe out the pirates in battles at sea had been unsuccessful.'

The blatant lies of history! As he was deploying his ships before Ulcinj, *General Providur* Daniel Dolfino IV thought back to the day his uncle told him Fra Dolcino's secret. His uncle had spoken slowly, and he, still a boy, had stared wide-mouthed and absorbed every word. The air around them had burned on that serene, summer day, just like today, when he and his army were finally so close to the book he'd sworn to retake for Christendom.

The *General Providur* believed he'd find the book hidden in the wall of the church which the infidel had turned into a mosque. When the monastery by Bojana River had been destroyed, one of the Franciscan friars, who knew Dolcino's secret, had taken the book and hidden it in the church in Ulcinj's Old Town. But Ulcinj fell to the Mohammedans. *Today people captured on pirate raids are sold as slaves in the church square,* Daniel Dolfino thought with disgust. *And there, overlooking the square, is the tower where the Jewish prophet who became a Mohammedan lived until his death. Pah, work of the infidel!* With God's aid, order would soon be returned to that part of the world: shipping in the Adriatic would be free of the infidel threat, Ulcinj would be Christian again, and he would finally get hold of the book which had fired his imagination for so many years – the book he believed to contain the answers to so many questions humanity could only ask with fear.

It's noon, and a mistral from the sea fills the sails of the Venetian ships. Standing beside the general, I can see the deadly determination in his eyes. *Fire!* he commands his troops.

The siege of Ulcinj lasted almost one month. In the end, the Venetian troops re-boarded their ships and returned to the Bay of Kotor. They'd managed to take the town of Ulcinj and well nigh raze it to the ground; they'd also blocked off the aqueduct. But the pirate stronghold had not fallen.

Rain beat against the windows of the Venetian headquarters in Perast. In the library, *General Providur* Daniel Dolfino wrote his report to his superiors: 'We were unable to take Ul-

84

cinj, but if the main goal was to punish the audacity and arrogance of the pirates, we have at least taught them a lesson.' History books would describe his campaign as a partial success. But he alone knew how immense and utter his defeat was. All the honour and glory of this world would be worthless to him after that. Until the end of his earthly days he'd dream of the former church – now a mosque – up in the unassailable Ulcinj fortress; he'd dream of opening the book whose words would take him by the hand and lead him to where only the elect may go.

Back in his Smyrna days, Zevi arrived at the idea that all books and human knowledge are not only superfluous but a diabolical burden on humanity's shoulders. He was completely obsessed by this idea during his ten-year stay in Ulcinj. Knowledge, he told his followers, prevents us from hearing the clear message of God. We may thus assume that Zevi was familiar with the teachings of Thomas Müntzer. '*Bibel, Bubel, Babel* – Bible-babble and Babylon: all that clutter has to be discarded so we can turn directly to God,' Müntzer wrote. 'The scholars think it's sufficient to read the Word of God in books and spit it out raw, like a stork spits out frogs for its young in the nest.'

Müntzer was Luther's student: a brilliant intellectual who burned with hatred towards everything that in the slightest way resembled intellect. Not inappropriately, they dubbed him the *Apostle of the Ignorant*. In his reckoning with books, Müntzer elevated the illiterate masses to authorised expositors of Scripture. The weakening of the authority of the Catholic Church also weakened its Truth, which at that time was the backbone of the world. Now, in place of that backbone, doomsday movements embedded implants fashioned in smithies and sheds, forests and caves. Their peg-legged Truth was crooked, crippled and lame. The common people took the matter into their own hands and Europe was ravaged by myriad groups guided by grotesquely distorted ideas. The people intervened in the corpus of the Christian idea, carrying out their operations with butcher-like precision. After this surgery by the 'popular experts', Christian Europe resembled Frankenstein. All across Europe, cities blazed, outlaw communities replaced liturgy with sexual perversions, cannibalism took over from Communion in places, and the ground was soaked with blood. Under the rule of millenarians, one contemporary wrote, 'the world is awash in a torrent of blood which will rise as high as a horse's head'.

Unlike Müntzer, who rejected all books, Zevi recommended the world one title – the one he himself authored and titled *The Book of the Coming.* But it will only be read when he arises and brings the Truth. For the interim, he left a fake book in this world of lies: *The Glory of the Return*, which he wrote by candlelight during the long nights in his tower, before the Star of David. Zevi considered that this book, which explains his teachings and the future of his people, contains just about as much truth as the world can bear. He bequeathed a difficult task to his followers, who would pass his words from mouth to mouth through many generations up until today: they must destroy his fake book, as well as that of the false messiah Fra Dolcino, before he can return and bring with him the real Holy Book. His followers had to find and burn those two books, otherwise his coming would be prevented and his people would continue to roam the world without peace and without a home.

Zevi left Ulcinj in the same way he arrived – spectacularly. Back when he disembarked on the beach below the fortress, black birds had risen up to meet him. On his last day he was strolling through the town in the company of two followers. They came across a group of people gathered around a fig tree, crying. A woman held in her arms a lifeless boy who'd fallen out of the tree. Then Zevi said: 'O Lord, send back this child and take me instead!' The boy opened his eyes and started to cry, while Zevi fell down dead on the cobbles. As the people lifted up his body and bore it away in wonder and gratitude, a murder of crows circled above them.

Now you know it all. The Ulcinj Library was burned down because Dolcino's book lay hidden there among all the worthless titles. Daniel Dolfino IV had been right – Dolcino's book really was hidden in the wall of the former church, now a mosque, in the Old Town. Workers renovating the church after the cataclysmic earthquake of 1979 found it, after which it was kept at the Ulcinj Library. The staff there didn't know its value and consigned it to a depot for old books no one wanted.

About a hundred of Zevi's followers had gone with him to Ulcinj. Although they'd all formally adopted Islam, in their hearts they'd never renounced Judaism. After Zevi's death, they scattered to all parts of the world: some returned to Smyrna, while others went as far away as Australia. They in turn died, but their descendants learned to preserve the secret of their faith about what lay buried in the hill cemetery above Ulcinj. Where did the devotees come from to carry out their assignment and await the coming of the Messiah? Who'll ever know? – perhaps from Turkey, where they're called Dönmeh, or from

California, where Yakov Leib HaKohain of Galata in Istanbul went to gather the faithful and prepare them for Zevi's return.

When Zevi had felt his end drawing near, he crept out of the fortress and climbed up to the cemetery with a group of his disciples. There his *Book of the Coming* was buried in a tomb, following ancient rites. The Messiah would thus have his Holy Book nearby when he arose at his burial place in Ulcinj.

Zevi's fake book, *The Glory of the Return*, was stolen from the house of the Vukotićs, who'd bought it at auction in London. Zevi's followers are fiendishly cunning: they burned down an entire library to cover up their burning of one book. And in order to conceal their theft of the other, they killed an entire family and left misleading clues.

From the Vukotićs', they went straight to the old Jewish cemetery where *The Book of the Coming* lay waiting in deep, sylvan oblivion. There, on the grave of Zevi's true book, they performed a ritual according to rules laid down by the Messiah himself and burned his fake script.

The first book had been destroyed in the library fire. The second was burned at the cemetery. The third was now dug out of its tomb: the Messiah could come again.

Chapter Seven

*in which we briefly enter a public house, venture into a dark marsh
and hear of self-pity and grace as Lazar tells his story; we meet
singing nuns, and a company of drunken friends confess their sins*

What drove Lazar to kill the Vukotićs that evening? Or
rather: what stopped him from killing them *before*
that?

If I hadn't lived through the war here, I wouldn't know.
But I saw what happens when the safety net of social relations
fails and social masks are dropped – when *the truth about us*
gets out. I saw the collapse of the world in which we'd played
our little roles as good people and friendly neighbours. Like
when a dam bursts, the water floods through, and the peaceful valley of the world we knew is suddenly swamped by the
deluge of our desires. All the dead of the wars of the 1990s
are a bodycount of the fantasies and deepest desires of our
neighbours and fellow human beings.

A man lives with his neighbours in 'peace and harmony' for
decades. Ask anyone in the local area about him and they'll
tell you he's a peaceful, friendly guy. Isn't the crime news in
the papers always the same? Don't people always describe
their neighbour in the same way, and then – out of the blue
– he commits a terrible, bloodthirsty crime? He conforms to
social conventions for years and years. But then comes a day

when he follows his own desires: he goes into the house of people he's lived alongside in peace and love for decades and kills them all. Who is the man living next door? Who is the criminal from our wars? An *ordinary man*, a good neighbour of forty years' standing, who under the sway of ideology, religion or whatever, blows a fuse and commits the crime? No: he's a killer who wished to see his neighbours dead for forty years and one day finally did what he'd *always wanted*.

It's the same with *sincere* friends. My good friend is drunk: he comes up to me and insults me; he tells me he despises me – no, he hates me, a hatred I deserve for things I've done, some of them in the distant, common past, which he enumerates and describes with what feels like the inhuman precision of a surveillance device. When I see him again the next day, he stands before me with his head bowed and apologises. 'Please forgive me, I was drunk,' he says.

What is my friend actually apologising for? Not for what he thinks and feels, but for having *said* what he thinks. He apologises for truth having punctured the condom of interpersonal consideration under the influence of alcohol. His apology is a request for me to reject the obvious: yes, that is what he really thinks about me. Hypocrisy is at the very heart of so-called good interpersonal relations. It's the very core of our everyday forgiveness. Usually we forgive what is done to us and manage to ignore the fundamental question of *why* it was done to us. Even if we forgive from the position of a good Christian, we do so in the full knowledge that there's a final arbiter, our God, who considers the claim for clemency once again. What's more, we forgive in full awareness that we have to forgive for our own sins to be forgiven. So that the outcome of the trial in which we are being judged be favourable, we have to relinquish our authority in the trial where we are the judge and transfer the matter to the 'Supreme Court'. We forgive, fully aware of the existence of the Heavenly Bank of Sin, in which every transgression counts. Our interests in the Bank of Sin render us fundamentally incapable of forgiving: a person can only truly forgive if their grace is disinterested. Ours never is, therefore it isn't grace.

*

One of the Vukotićs' neighbours told me he'd seen Lazar drunk several times at the Lonely Hearts bar, where I didn't go because it was frequented by the local working class. An essential precondition for joining the struggle for the rights of the working class is that you not know the working class. After all, ignorance is the precondition for every struggle: as soon as we get to know something well, we can no longer imagine fighting for it.

The local proletarians met at the Lonely Hearts to dream of better days and drink away their wages. Despite the flood and snowstorm, the place was packed that night. The owner of the Lonely Hearts was nicknamed Pasha. No one remembered his real name any more. He was a petty crook from Bosnia who came to Ulcinj like so many others to escape the war. The natives of Ulcinj are wise: they know that current adversities will be replaced by the adversities to come. One occupier will replace another – one despot will be deposed by the next. This makes them paragons of patience, in no hurry to replace their current misfortune with the next in the sequence of misfortunes. In fact, if the misfortune lasts long enough you become so used to it that you can't imagine your life without it. The natives of Ulcinj know how to get on with people like Pasha: they let them live next door and just don't allow their bars, quarrels and shams to affect their lives.

Pasha owed me a favour, like many other people in town. His problem was that he treated people like idiots. That's not a bad basis for success in life, in principle, as long as you're not an idiot yourself. Pasha was.

Things were bound to blow up in his face sooner or later. I made sure he survived the blast. Therefore, when I entered the Lonely Hearts, I expected that I'd just need to do a bit of the mandatory, folksy *not-on-your-life-mate* haggling, and that Pasha would then tell me where to find Lazar.

In 1999, long lines of Kosovar refugees poured into Ulcinj, fleeing from the Serbian troops or NATO's bombs. Many of these displaced people dreamed of making it to Europe. Pasha offered to help them achieve that dream.

Serious criminals sailed from Montenegrin harbours for Italy in boats full of refugees. Some of the vessels made it to the other side of the Adriatic, others sank and took with them many a dream of good wages, second-hand Mercedes and savings for building garishly painted villas near Prizren and Priština with decorative plaster lions on the balconies.

Of all the human traffickers, Pasha was the cheapest. This was partly because he operated with the lowest overheads and partly because people paid him to take them to Italy – but he didn't take them there. Pasha would load his clients into a truck and cart them through Montenegro all night: from Ulcinj to Kolašin, from Kolašin to Nikšić, from Nikšić to

Risan, then round the Bay of Kotor, via Budva, and back to Ulcinj. The others all used boats, but he stuck to good old terra firma, Pasha boasted. At dawn he'd unload the people on the sandy beach of Bojana Island near Ulcinj, at the southernmost tip of Montenegro. The refugees looked around in confusion because they couldn't see a single structure or anything that might have confirmed to them that they were really in Italy. 'Just keep walking a bit, and when you meet someone, wish them *Buon giorno*!' Pasha instructed them, before hopping back into the truck and speeding off.

The refugees would roam along the beach with suitcases in hand until they came across a local watchman who, to their astonishment, would reply to their *Buon giorno* with obscenities in Albanian.

Pasha's plan had only one flaw: it overlooked what would happen next. The refugees would realise he'd ripped them off and would then have no other goal in life than to kill him. I'm a well-informed man: as soon as I heard they were after Pasha I sent him to a friend's place in Bar, where he hid until the furious refugees had returned to Kosovo.

While I waited for Pasha to familiarise some new female staff with the house rules, I realised that the Lonely Hearts had extended its range: along with the terrible drink, guests could now pay for hideously ugly prostitutes. One of them, a wench with part blonde, part black hair and a few missing teeth, offered me the services of one of the *beautiful girls*, she emphasised.

'No thanks, I've already got a full collection of STDs,' I said.

'Then at least buy me a drink,' she insisted. She was obviously thirsty, and a gentleman always helps a damsel in distress.

'Aren't you the local Sherlock Holmes?' she asked as she was quaffing her brandy.

'More like Philip Marlowe,' I corrected her. 'Holmes keeps women at an arm's length, whereas Marlowe takes them under his wing, only to destroy them later.'

'I love Holmes films,' she avowed, determined to continue our cultured conversation. 'What I like most is when he shows how clever he is: you know, when he just looks at someone, and the next instant he can tell you everything about them after having seen just a few details, which only he has noticed. Can you do that too?' she wondered.

'I could give it a try,' I said. 'Since you don't stink of sweat like the other whores in this joint, I infer you weren't working today. Therefore I assume Pasha has set you aside for himself because only his mistresses are entitled to days off. I see you've swabbed two inches of powder on your face and also note that you've washed your hair. That means you want to appeal to Pasha and be attractive for him. That, in turn, means that you hope to stay his mistress. Who knows, with a bit of luck he might even marry you. After all, doesn't every man ultimately want to settle down with a good woman by his side? But that's not going to happen: even if we live to see tomorrow, the day will bring a girl younger than you. Then Pasha will give you the boot. You're afraid of that, and it's on your mind. Warm?'

'You have no idea,' she snorted and demonstratively relieved me of her company. I wouldn't want to sound pretentious, but I'm pretty sure I managed to drive her to tears.

Half an hour later I was in the boat, passing what remained

of the petrol station. Pasha had done me a favour: I now knew that Lazar lived in one of the stilt houses on Saltern Canal and had done so ever since coming to Ulcinj.

The canal had once been navigable. When King Nicholas of Montenegro captured Ulcinj, he named the canal Port Milena in honour of his wife. Princely sailboats would moor there. The establishment of the nearby salt works turned the canal into a giant fish pond because the salt it released into the water attracted the fish. Dozens of stilt houses sprang up on the canal; local fisherfolk would lower nets into the water, and when they raised them again they were full of catch. Later the canal devolved into a cesspool because the houses which grew up all around discharged their sewage straight into it. Soon there were no more fish in the canal. The people left too. Punting on the canal had once been a favourite pastime of the Montenegrin royal family. Now going to the canal meant venturing deep into a marsh.

My trusty boat cut the calm water, which was topped with floating pieces of furniture from submerged houses. Two crows were riding on the carcass of a cow and blithely pecking at its entrails. Drowned people drifted past, too, their bodies grotesquely rounded like blow-up dolls. I pulled my scarf over my face and tried not to inhale the stench. Whenever the boat bumped into them I'd use the oar to push aside those bodies – their hearts now home to beetles and worms, not love – and then continued on my way. Just like a slice of bread always falls butter-side down, drowned people always float with their face in the water, it occurred to me.

I paddled along the former boulevard leading to Velika Plaža. The roof of a truck protruded from the water in the parking lot in front of the shopping centre. There had been no power in the region for weeks. The metal lamp-posts swayed in the wind. The billboards still announced summer fun: a buxom singer performed on a terrace by the sea, a tanned brunette advertised sun cream promising protection from skin cancer, and there was a new line of fruit ice cream which *took care of your children's teeth*. I passed abandoned auto repair shops and bakeries. Restaurant terraces where cheerful tourists had bobbed and skipped to folk dances from home were now swimming pools for ducks.

Large snowflakes descended silently from the dark sky. It was frigid in the marsh, the kind of damp cold which really gets into your bones. People kept saying this was the cold of the End, but I remember well the cold of the beginning, from my childhood. On the coldest of winter days, when the salt works' canals turned to ice, I'd go there to hunt ducks. I'd creep through the snow-covered dunes and, small as I was, hide in the reeds around the edges of the frozen ponds. I tied rags or strips of hessian around my boots. That allowed me to run on the ice and gave me a decisive advantage – it made the hunt possible in the first place. A duck on the ice is slow. It has trouble taking off because it needs a run-up, which is difficult on the ice, and its clumsy legs let it down. A duck on the ice is like Ollie in the Laurel and Hardy films: fat and ungainly. It falls over a few times before getting the forward motion needed to take off, and that gave me the chance to reach it and kill it with my stick. I remember the duck would sometimes get airborne, and then I'd hit it with my stick like a baseball player slams the ball.

A lamp was on in one of the stilt houses – like a lighthouse showing me the way, I thought. I turned off the motor, trying to sneak up on Lazar unnoticed.

I found father and son there in the small, cluttered space, huddled up to an old woodstove. The old man was sitting in an ancient armchair with springs sticking out, one of those communist replicas of 1950s American design which were once used to furnish hotels on the coast.

He sat there calmly, like Abraham Lincoln in his Washington memorial.

'He's blind and deaf – he has been for twenty years,' Lazar said in a low voice.

But the old man was nodding to a rhythm only he could hear.

'I know who you are, and I know why you've come,' Lazar whispered. 'I've been expecting you. The police or someone else. As soon as I killed them I knew I'd be punished. I'm not afraid of punishment. Look where I live and how I live. Punish me – it'll be my salvation.'

I sat down on a stool close to the stove to warm my frozen toes. I pulled the bottle out of my coat pocket and took a good swig.

'Why did you do it?' I demanded.

'The real truth, sir, is that I don't know. Back then I thought I knew: I was furious and felt I had to kill them all that instant. But when I look back at what I did, and I have time to look back at my actions – what else is there to do here? – I realise I didn't have a reason. At least none which people would understand.'

'Still, if we tried, you'd be surprised what I can understand,' I encouraged him.

He explained that he'd come to Ulcinj from Vojvodina in northern Serbia, where he'd lived with his family and his father.

'It feels like he's always been old,' he said, pointing at his father. 'Look at him: can you believe he was once young?!'

Back home, in the plains of Central Europe, Lazar had been a repair man: people would call him, and he'd go and get their things running again.

'It was an honest job, but honest jobs don't earn much money. I got used to poverty, and I always knew I'd die poor. But my family wanted more, so I became the scapegoat for their *miserable lives*, as they called them. Have you ever felt the contempt of your own children?' he asked. 'Do you know what it's like when your children say to your face that you're a *loser, a coward, a weakling, a sucker*? That your father is *an old vampire who refuses to die and make us happy*? For days on end, even on Sundays, I'd be rushing from house to house, eternally tired and dirty, but that wasn't good enough for them. No sirree, they always wanted more. My father and I became unwelcome in our own home – the house I'd built with my own hands.

'That's why we left. I'd heard there was a lot of building going on in Montenegro on the coast and that tradesmen were in demand, so we moved here. And it worked out: I got a job at a building site. We were doing well, me and the old man. Until I took a fall from the scaffolding. Now I'm lame in one leg and drag it behind me like a club-foot. There are lots of strapping young men looking for work, so who needs an old limper?

'Just when I thought I couldn't earn a crust here any

more – just when it looked like the two of us would have to hit the road again – the Vukotićs gave me a job. Madam Vukotić opened the gate and immediately took pity on me. She asked me inside, gave me a good meal, and I started work there the very next day. She was a kind woman, Senka – soft-hearted, and that went to her head. It's not good to pity people. Don't mind me saying so, but you look like someone who understands that. It's not good even to pity oneself. I'm inclined to self-pity, you see, and that's really made my life hell. It's a great evil: I've killed people, but I still feel sorry for myself.

'We moved into this stilt house here. How should I put it – it's not exactly five-star luxury, but at least it's rent-free. My pay at the Vukotićs' was substantial. We lacked nothing, and we two old boys could have gone on like that for years. But I kept thinking about my wife and children and the house, as much as I tried not to; every night my thoughts flew back to Vojvodina and I'd cry the whole night through when I thought what grief and injustice had befallen me. It was driving me nuts, and I started drinking and gambling at the Lonely Hearts . . . You know how it is: when you gamble drunk you lose, and then you need another drink.

'My pay at the Vukotićs' was good, like I said. But I needed more, and the Vukotićs had enough. I thought I could take from them without them noticing. A little for them was a lot for me.

'So I stole from them. Nothing big, you know: a tenner or twenty from the purse Senka used to leave on the kitchen table when she came back from shopping and went up to her room to get changed. A vase or two, or a piece of jewellery.

99

'One day when I was painting the tool shed Senka brought me out a cold glass of lemonade. And then she said nonchalantly, like just in passing: "I'd ask you not to steal from us any more." She didn't wait for an answer but simply turned and went back into the house.

'That night I thought I'd die of shame. There was no one for me to confide in, so I sat here with my deaf father almost through till dawn, even though he was mostly sleeping in his armchair like he's drowsing now, and wrung out my heart. I'd become a good-for-nothing in the eyes of the people who'd been so good to me, people whose kindness meant we still had work and a roof over our heads and weren't forced to wander the world in misery as a cripple and a geriatric.

'I tried to apologise to Senka and promised it wouldn't happen again. She told me with a compassion which hurt, as if I was a lowly creature crawling the earth, that no explanation was needed and that she knew very well what extremes people can be driven to by poverty. She said she didn't hold anything against me and that, as far as she was concerned, nothing had happened: "We've taken you in and decided to help you – we'll give you another chance."

'But not one month had passed, and I took to stealing again. The Lonely Hearts may be the cheapest bar in town but it was still too expensive for me. This time Senka invited me into the house, served me some chocolate cake, and then raked me over the coals in front of the whole family: although they'd already forgiven me once, I kept on stealing from them. They were disappointed, she said, but they realised I had it hard and knew I'd have nowhere to go if they gave up on me, so they wouldn't send me away. But I should be aware that it was *truly deplorable* how low I'd fallen – those were the words she used.

'Instead of vexation and regret, this time I felt anger. When they saw me out into the garden and Senka gave me instructions for mowing the lawn, I was brimming with hatred towards her. Yes, they'd helped me when I was in a tight spot. But did that give them the right to humiliate me, what's more in front of the children? I often told stories to them about the olden days and they seemed truly happy listening to them. What would the children think of me now? *My transgression is one thing. Please punish me, Madam Vukotić* – I seethed inside as I turned on the lawnmower, *but don't put me down in front of the children. Perhaps you think I'm so wretched that I don't even deserve punishment. Is that what you want to say, that even punishment is too good for me? Don't those who are punished, even those who are punished most harshly (especially them!) warrant a modicum of respect? Don't those who are punished at least regain their dignity in the end? Isn't it a terrible crime to rob the punished of their human dignity, bigger by all means than the one I committed in stealing? Did you employ me to work for you, Madam Vukotić, or for you to practise your kindliness on me? When I trudge off home in the evenings, do you stand in front of the mirror and admire your own virtue?'* Lazar foamed with rage, squirming in his chair.

'I kept on working as best I could. I pruned the orchard, hoed the garden, repaired the water heaters and pipes, but I was determined not to put up with any more humiliation. For days on end I quietly practised a speech to give to Senka, one she'd *have to* listen to. Oh yes: no one would interrupt Lazar mid-sentence any more. *You have my gratitude but that doesn't mean you can look down on me. I work for you, but I'm not a lesser human being,* I was going to tell her.

'One day I was in the tool shed making a new handle for the axe, when she popped in to look for an improvised watering can. "Madam Vukotić –," I spoke in as decisive a voice as I could muster. "Not now, Lazar!" she snuffed, rummaging on the shelf. Fed up with everything and white-hot with anger, I stormed up to her and grabbed her by the arm. She wheeled around abruptly: I felt her sweet breath on my face, and the tips of her large breasts brushed me.

'She hadn't expected this. For the first time since we'd known each other it wasn't pity she felt. I could see fear in her eyes. *What now? What's he going to do to me?* she was thinking.

'For a few seconds I stood before her, proud, enjoying that superiority. Then she pushed me aside, moved away, and declared in that same condescending, matronly tone, which drives me mad even now when I think about it, that her husband wouldn't find out what had just happened. I should be ashamed of myself. She hadn't expected this from me, but she'd forgive me one more time. As she left, she added: "You don't need to worry about your job. You're a walking disaster – you don't need punishment when you've got yourself."

'I left their property, determined never to go back again. I sat and drank at the Lonely Hearts until evening, muttering to myself: *Lazar may be poor, but he still has pride. He'll make sure no lady looks down on him again.*

'Drunk, humiliated and livid with rage, I went back up the hill to their property. I had the key to the gate, so I entered the grounds without being seen. I took my tools from the shed: knife, spade and axe. I put my work gloves on. When I look back at that night, I don't think I intended to kill anyone. I just wanted respect. But why then did I put the gloves on, you may ask? I have no answer to that, at least none people would understand. I rang the doorbell, determined to speak my mind to Senka, say thank-you for her kindness and leave with my head held high.

'I had to ring three times before she came down and opened the door. As soon as she saw me, the browbeating began: I'd really gone too far now. Did I know what time it was? I couldn't wake them this late, and I was drunk as well. She told me to go home and sleep it off, and they'd decide what to do with me the next day. I tried to speak, but she went on and on, bombarding me with words which came down on my head like a hammer.

'I shut my eyes and swung the axe,' he said.

'But the children and her husband: why them?' I asked.

'They were woken by the noise. If only I'd killed her with the first blow . . . But she staggered and knocked over the vase before falling to the floor. It smashed damn loudly, like a gunshot. That's what woke them. It's all because of the vase that they're now dead.

'Pavle was at the stairs and saw me kill her. He went for the shotgun. I had no choice. I had to go all the way and get rid of them all,' he said calmly. 'I'm pedantic – when I start a job I always finish it. Then I removed all the traces, or so I thought. I threw the knife into the marsh. Only then, drunk with alcohol and blood, did I realise that I'd forgotten the axe. Since then I've been living in anticipation of the police coming to get me.

'It was hardest with Helena. I'd got on with her the best, and I'll miss her the most. I took her to the couch and switched on the television for her. She liked watching programmes about animals. I sat down beside her and, to tell you the truth, I started to cry,' Lazar said.

I lit a cigarette and knocked back a good swig from my bottle. I looked at the old man. He muttered in his sleep and his dry lips moved quickly. It looked like he was praying.

'Are you going to take me to the police station now?' Lazar asked.

'She was right,' I said.

'Who?'

'That woman, Senka – she was right: we don't need punishment when we've got ourselves.'

On the way out I turned to look at them once more: the killer and his old father by the stove. 'How much money did you take from the safe?' I asked.

'What safe?' Lazar replied, startled, as if shaken from deep thought. 'The Vukotićs were prudent: they kept their money in the bank. If there was a safe in the house, I didn't know about it.'

I got back into the boat and left the marsh as quickly as I could. Like people say, trouble never comes alone. As if the cold and the snow blowing in my face weren't enough to make me miserable, I'd run out of whisky. I disembarked at the town council building's parking lot, broke into the first café and deposited a bottle of Jameson in my coat pocket. I stood in the dark, leaning against the bar, calmly watching Christmas turn the streets white. Many people had turned off the lights in their houses. They stood at the windows waiting, or knelt by their beds and prayed for mercy. Maybe they lay with the blankets over their heads and talked about the past. I went round behind the bar, poured myself a drink and switched on the radio. A witty DJ put on the Sex Pistols and Johnny Rotten screamed *No Future*. I looked at my face in the mirror and sent myself a sincere, warm smile. *Fucking hell, those were good times,* I sighed.

Then my phone rang and shattered my moment of nostalgia like a harbinger of doom. Dragan Vukotić still wanted to avenge his dead brother. What should I tell him – that I had Lazar, and he was longing to be punished? That I had an excellent story with just one unresolved detail: a safe, whose existence I couldn't vouch for because the house had burned down? No thanks, I thought, and hurled the phone out into the snow. I went outside. A howling came from the maternity hospital: a dog had been shut inside and now stood in the dark amongst the empty cradles yowling for someone, anyone, to come.

A group of nuns stood at the traffic lights and called on the occasional passers-by to embrace Christianity. 'Accept Jesus now, the End is nigh!' they shouted. It was like when market stallholders yell, *It's all gotta go!* The group had a well-defined division of labour: some did the hard sell for salvation while the others sang. Their song brought a lot of things home to me, like that they'd actually had no choice but to join the monastery. They certainly wouldn't have made it as a rock band, I told them.

'You mean you don't believe *even today*?!' I was asked by the most inquisitive – or maybe the stupidest.

'No,' I said, 'but you know how it is: I will as soon as I get cancer.'

Our parting feelings for each other couldn't exactly have been called love. Each of them spat after me three times and then hurriedly crossed themselves. Dealing with an old-fashioned gentleman like me is one thing, I thought, but what are they going to do about these fellows who are at least as fervent as them? Six bearded men strode angrily towards them, gesticulating aggressively and going ballistic with umbrage.

As they passed me, heading for the nuns, one of them pointed to the Jameson I was carrying: 'That's *haram* – you'll burn in hell!' he promised.

'Cheers,' I seconded.

If any pub is open tonight, it'll be Johnny's, I reckoned. I got into the car. It started up straight away. Then the shape of a man emerged from the snow, approaching with mighty strides. It was Salvatore.

'Get in,' I told him.

'How are you tonight?' he asked politely.

'Same as ever. When you look at it, it's a day like any other, don't you think?'

'I was up at your place. When I didn't find you, I told myself to go for a walk through town, thinking that perhaps I'd meet you. And there you go: I run smack bang into you. It's a small world. Anyway, you know why I'm looking for you. I thought that by now you could perhaps tell me who killed my son, and why. My wife is waiting for me at home – it's she who sent me to look for you. She said: "Go and ask him so at least we can wait in peace for whatever this night will bring."'

There was nothing for it, I had to improvise. Salvatore listened in silence as I explained what I'd learned: his son had been killed by a madman – an escapee from a mental hospital in Kotor:

'The doctors and nurses left the hospital and a horde of lunatics is now free to roam the country. I pursued the killer for days. Tonight I finally caught up with him in the marsh. It was either him or me. I couldn't get him to give himself up, so I had to shoot. He was swallowed up by the dark water. Now he's lying there somewhere in the mud.'

Salvatore buried his head in his hands and sobbed. 'I knew it,' he said after wiping away his tears. 'What sane person would do that to a child?'

'You can go home,' I told him. 'It's over. It's all over now. I've done what there was to be done. Go back and tell your wife that everything's in its place again.'

He shook my hand firmly and looked at me with tearful eyes full of gratitude. I watched him in the rear-view mirror running off through the blizzard to take the good news home.

I arrived at Johnny's just in time to witness a collective confession. My regular drinking mates were preoccupied with the looming Apocalypse, which they now took for granted. Alcohol was flowing in hectolitres and Johnny was handing out bottle after bottle from behind the bar without a break, obviously determined to have the pub drunk dry by the end of the evening. As they used to say in Partisan films: *Not one grain of wheat should be left for the invaders!* In this final hour, the drunken gang felt the need to let out its deepest secrets and worst sins. They demanded that Father Frano hear their confessions.

'I can't, guys: most of you aren't Catholic, let alone christened,' he said in his defence. This pragmatic country priest had come from Dalmatia thirty years ago and had had to learn quickly how to get on with the wily local flock which gathered in his church on Sundays. He knew that God had no need to listen to the garbage these drunkards would confess. 'We'll do it like this –,' he proposed, 'you'll confide in one another because the most important thing is to be frank with your neighbour and with yourself. God is satisfied with that.'

It really must be high time if even Catholic confessions have become like AA meetings, I thought.

Božo was the first to open up his heart. There was silence while he spoke, apart from the sound of clinking glasses. He made a dramatic pause after every act of adultery he admitted, and Father Frano gave him an indulgent look to embolden him to continue. When Božo finished, his listeners were mildly disappointed: infidelity, drunkenness and domestic violence – all in all, Božo had lived an ordinary, mainstream life.

Frowns crept over the men's faces when Zoran began to tell his sins: 'I'm a poof. Johnny will probably tell you himself when it's his turn, but he's one too: we've had something going for fifteen years. The wife and the kids don't suspect anything, neither mine nor his. I can see in your eyes that you condemn me. I knew it'd be like this, and that's why I never told you. Now you're probably asking yourselves: *How many times did the bugger look at my backside?* I know you are – there's no need to be ashamed. The answer is: not once. I want you to know that – you've always just been friends to me. Before you reject me, ask yourselves if I've ever betrayed you . . . Now that you know the truth, I just want to ask you one thing: please don't turn your back on me.'

An ambiguous request, to say the least! I'd always found him pretty unbearable: his macho pose, easy rider and cowboy boots – what a put-on! I could imagine him wearing red lace knickers under his leathers.

Then it got even worse: Fahro admitted that he'd been sleeping with Božo's wife for years. Even Father Frano seemed bewildered – he was obviously losing control of this little nightly collective confession. It was as if someone had opened Pandora's box and now people, one after another, were saying things which in different circumstances would cause friendships to be broken off and blood to flow.

When Johnny recounted having been raped by three young men at high school in Bar, Father Frano began to cry. Is there anything more unbearable than the moment when people *open up their heart*, as the expression goes? I'd rather watch open-heart surgery than be around at times like this when the toxic waste of human lives leaks out.

In tears, Father Frano described the day he stopped believing in God: 'Nothing spectacular happened that day, I just woke up in the morning and realised that I knew *nothing* about all the people I had advised on how to lead their lives. I didn't understand the souls I had to give pastoral care to, nor did I respect them. I was just the guy that peddled God,' he blubbered.

'That morning I opened my eyes and my whole dismal life flashed before me, right up to its unavoidably wretched end. But I didn't have the strength to throw off the cassock and put an end to the lies. Above all, I didn't have the courage to appear so naked before my family. My vocation as a priest was a great source of pride for them, and leaving the priesthood would definitely be the ultimate disgrace. I thought: if I tell the truth I'll hurt many, and if I keep lying I'll only destroy myself,' Frano said.

Fuck this life! Is this ordeal ever going to end? I screamed to myself. I downed shot after shot of whisky, getting absolutely plastered in the hope of falling unconscious from inebriation and escaping this hell of cheap sincerity – that bastard born of despair from an illicit liaison with fear.

Out of the corner of my eye, I saw Gogi kneel in front of Frano and lower his head into the priest's lap.

'I killed a man,' he said, and an icy draught flowed through the room. 'I've killed a man,' he repeated and stood up, tears running down his face. 'I've killed more than once,' he shouted, drawing a revolver from his pocket and pointing it at his temple.

I couldn't stay a second longer. I felt sick from all the whisky I'd drunk and all the repulsive things I'd heard.

'Stupid, bloody fools!' I yelled and stormed out into the blizzard. *Now everything's fallen apart, I've just lost all my friends.* As I was striding swiftly towards the car, I heard the shot. That was the seal on our doom.

Chapter Eight

in which we learn of an unhappy love affair and the deaths of
loved ones, Hedvige reveals to Emmanuel her last and greatest
secret, we hear of the cruel death of countless animals and are
overwhelmed with powerless remorse

from: emmanuel@gmail.com
to: thebigsleep@yahoo.com

Dr Schulz was particularly intrigued by my father being a detective. 'How interesting, how very interesting,' he muttered
into his beard as he paced in circles, gnawing on his pipe and
puffing at his vanilla-scented tobacco.

'You see, the desire for an Apocalypse is a sure sign of the
inability to cope with anxiety – the inevitable angst of waiting
for the endgame which we hope will provide an outcome and
an explanation. Not to mention the anxiety of waiting for an answer to the question: is there an outcome and an explanation
at all? This anxiety grows as we get closer to an answer and
as it becomes ever clearer that there is actually no answer.
When we desire an Apocalypse, we're instinctively reaching
for the remote control so we can fast-forward through our own
life history to the end, like we might do with a gripping detective film. It's like we can no longer resist the urge to find out
who committed the crime,' Dr Schulz said.

'God the Father, who brings the Apocalypse, does the same as the sleuth at the end of a well-crafted detective story. At the end, God assembles all those involved in the crime – and what is history but a crime story with humanity as its cast? He gathers everyone together, be they now living or dead, and explains the role of each character in turn: he discloses their hidden motives and intentions, exonerates the innocent, brandmarks the guilty, reveals the truth and clarifies the meaning of every seemingly senseless move by each of the actors. When a good sleuth and God are finished, no further interpretation is possible, there's only applause,' Dr Schulz exclaimed and clapped his hands loudly because he'd noticed that my thoughts had wandered off.

When he was in a good mood or I'd done or said something to arouse his intellectual curiosity, which must have been simply irrepressible in his younger days, Dr Schulz would launch into a long monologue. Of all the days I've spent in this asylum – where I'm confined *for my own good,* they never forget to say – I best remember those when Dr Schulz held one of his inspired discourses.

'Do you want to hear about the funny side of the end of the world?' he asked me once, and, in his usual way, continued without waiting for my reply. I swallowed his words avidly as he spoke about the apocalyptic prophecy pronounced by the Montanists in the second century AD. The sect was founded in 156 AD by Montanus, a prophet who seems to have had the ability to speak in unintelligible languages. This phenomenon has virtually become part of pop culture today: we know it under the name 'speaking in tongues' and it's an everyday practice in Pentecostal churches. It's also common in mental

112

institutions, where we call it schizophrenia. In any case, Jesus had scarcely gone, but Montanus believed he'd soon come again. The prophet wrongly predicted the date of Christ's return, but his cult lived on for several centuries.

'Elipando, Bishop of Toledo, described the uproar which took hold of the city's inhabitants on 6 April 793. He wrote that a monk by the name of Beatus, a manic street preacher, called the people together on the main square and told them the end of the world was coming that same evening. The city was panic-stricken. Later, when the people realised that the End hadn't occurred, they were enraged and went on a spree of plundering.

'Who better than the Pope to answer the question *When's the next time round?*' Dr Schulz laughed loudly. 'Pope Innocent III was unequivocal: the Second Coming would occur in 1284, that being 666 years after the advent of Islam. Jesus didn't come, despite the Pope's authority. Since the Pope was infallible, by inference Christ himself must have been wrong.

'Botticelli couldn't resist Apocalypse forecasting either. On a painting completed in 1500, he added a caption in Greek saying that the great cataclysm was coming in three and a half years: "Satan will be chained and cast down, as in this picture."

'Martin Luther believed the End would come by 1600. Tommaso Campanella was even more precise: the Earth would collide with the sun in 1603,' Dr Schulz said.

'Isaac Newton devoted a large part of his life and thought, which was not only mathematical but also theological, to the attempt to find what he considered the Bible code. And ultimately he succeeded, as he himself asserted. In 2003, the media were all abuzz about hitherto unpublished writings by Newton which state that the end of the world will come in 2060.

'The *London Stories about the End*, if I may call them that, are especially cheerful and bring out the British sense of humour,' Dr Schulz explained and refilled his pipe. 'In June 1523, a handful of London astrologers calculated that the end of the world would be on 1 February of the following year. It would begin with a flood in London. The water would then cover the entire world. Tens of thousands of people left their homes, fleeing before the predicted deluge. When the day of the prophecy came, not a drop of rain fell in London.

'The prophet William Bell said there would be a devastating earthquake on 5 April 1761 which would destroy the world. Previously he'd predicted a quake for 8 February. "So it didn't occur, but don't worry – it'll be on 8 March," he assured his listeners. Oops, wrong again. People left their homes and took to the hills yet again on 5 April, and when there was still no earthquake, an angry mob threw Bell into the London madhouse, Bethlem.

'In his *Book of Prophecies,* Christopher Columbus wrote that the world was created in 5343 BC and would last for 7,000 years. The End would therefore come in 1658. He got it wrong, but what can you expect of a man who was searching for India and discovered America?' Dr Schulz gibed.

He wasn't always in such a good mood. There were days, oh there certainly were, when he was gloomy and almost inscrutable. The warm laughter which had resounded in his study the day before would unexpectedly switch to a cold keenness, a presence almost like a scalpel, and I felt he could dissect me with his thoughts if he wanted.

And again, there were moments when he seemed to truly sympathise with me, when a story I told him in confidence shook him more than I thought a person in his position was allowed to be shaken. Sometimes I felt he sympathised with me so completely and sincerely that *I* suddenly had the desire to help *him*, as paradoxical as it may sound. Gentle and pensive, he'd listen to me without interrupting with a single gesture as I told him about my love for Marushka.

I was in love with Marushka even before I met her. One day Hedvige dropped her wallet and it fell under the sink. When I stooped down to get it, I saw her picture on the floor. She was my age, pallid of face and ethereally beautiful. I knew from what Hedvige had told me that she was of fragile health and that her chronic bronchitis had developed into asthma at an early age.

I often imagined her coughing blood and holding up a snow-white embroidered handkerchief in her slender fingers. There was something compellingly romantic for me in that scene of beauty separated from death by a single strand of maiden's hair. I'd always be there to keep her from falling. I'd bring up a chair and offer her a glass of water. She'd then raise her angelic blue eyes to me and, not letting go of my hand, say: *thank you*. The love between us couldn't last for long. Her illness would tear her away from me, I imagined, and for that very reason I was convinced that she was the love of my life: the only love I'd have would be unhappy, but I'd fling myself into that tragedy like the Spartans charged the Persian hordes.

We met at the Amarcord brassiere, where I used to go in my late teenager days to watch the tumult of Naschmarkt. This marketplace had exercised a magnetic pull on me even as a child. It was strictly off-limits for me, needless to say. Yet how many times had I toured Naschmarkt wide-eyed, absorbing every nuance of the fruit and vegetables on display, every wrinkle on the faces of the dark-skinned porters and the fat saleswomen with their stentorian laughs and wide, aproned bellies which looked like they were hiding kangaroos. Amidst all those sounds, colours and not always pleasant smells, I felt a heady excitement such as only comes over us on the greatest of adventures – asail on the most distant oceans, braving the most perilous battlefields and scaling the highest mountain peaks. My heart beat like a tin drum whenever one of the saleswomen leaned towards me and spoke to me in her poor German. What a treasury of stories Naschmarkt was for me! Green olives and white cheeses, smoked salmon and pickled legs of pork, dried figs from the Adriatic islands and dried tomatoes from Turkey, early cherries from Italy and late oranges from Egypt: every market stall had the power, like an invisible lock, to sluice me into a dangerous new world far away from Schikanedergasse. But you mustn't think I really wanted to travel to all those places: my journeys were so spectacular because of my confinement, and my confinement was so agreeable because of my journeys. Any change would only have disturbed that delicate equilibrium and would only have been for the worse.

As I mentioned, the Amarcord was directly opposite Naschmarkt. Here I'd drink Julius Meinl coffee, smoke and gaze out at that unofficial Vienna theatre of life, where I staged and played some of the most exciting episodes of my childhood. When Marushka got a job as a waitress at the Amarcord because Hedvige's wages working for us weren't enough to cover her education, I began dropping by every day. They served Guinness on tap and crispy roast duck in spicy orange sauce; everyone there knew me, from the cooks to the regular guests – failed artists who hung around all day in the alcoves, waylaying visitors careless enough to sit down at neighbouring tables and abusing them with tales of their 'new art projects'.

When Marushka and I left the Amarcord together for the first time and I accompanied her to St Stephen's Cathedral where she lit a candle on the anniversary of her grandmother's death; and when we sat in the Bräunerhof afterwards drinking tea; and when I took her to the bus stop; and when she gave me a kiss on the cheek before running to the bus – we knew our relationship was inconceivable for everyone else. And precisely for that reason it was the only conceivable one for me.

We were as discreet as only those can be who know that to be noticed means danger. The slightest carelessness on our part could have brought a torrent of adversities, because *maman et papa* weren't the only obstacle to our love: Hedvige would oppose it just as forcefully, if not more so. But I'd been good at keeping secrets since childhood – was I not Hedvige's pupil, after all?

And then, within less than a year, Marushka and I were left alone in the world. First of all my mother died. They searched all the way from Vienna to Thailand to find a cure for her illness, but in vain. She passed away in a Swiss clinic in 'the miraculous hands' of a quack who 'healed those whom the medical profession has written off', as the pamphlets claimed which kept turning up in our home for months after the funeral. Knowing my mother, I have no doubt that she believed until the very end that she'd come through it. She could never accept the idea that she'd die; even the possibility of ageing and of her beauty waning was unthinkable for her: off the edge of all mental maps, deep within the dark territory no thought would penetrate, because those who enter there must abandon all hope. Her mother was like that too – the grandmother whom I never met. Apparently she had the habit of saying: *If I should ever die . . .* My mother, keeping with her convictions, didn't write a will. *Papa* followed her example, which cost me a fortune in lawyers' fees over years of litigation with his relatives, who descended like a flock of vultures on his estate. Fortunately it was quite large. *Papa* was a weak but good man. And a good father, too – except that he wasn't my actual father.

Before long, Hedvige also died. After *papa* was buried, I insisted that she not leave – she was to stay and live with me in the apartment. At one stage I was determined that Marushka should move in too, but she energetically rejected the idea and forced me to repeat after her, for the umpteenth time: *My mother must never find out.* Hedvige did actually stay, but today I know it would've been better if she hadn't. She hovered about the apartment like a ghost. I'd find her polishing a piece of furniture endlessly, as if in a trance, and raining down tears on it. Poor *madame*, poor *monsieur,* she'd say all of a sudden at dinner and burst into tears. Everything in the apartment reminded her of them. Schikanedergasse became Hedvige's Calvary: the memories caused her great sorrow, and everything which still existed turned into a monument to the ephemeral. There was so much death all around: the neighbourhood changed, people died or moved away, and she no longer even knew the saleswomen at the local baker's. Everything that had been hers, except for Marushka and I, was now in the world of the dead. She didn't show it in any way, although it must have caused her pain, but *I know she knew* that we were no longer hers either. Then one day she joined the shadows she'd been living with in her last few months. She'd been with them in the other world for days on end, and it was only her body which periodically came back to us. So when she died she didn't go away: she just didn't come back.

Her death didn't bind me and Marushka together. After they'd all been buried, you might have thought that nothing more could stand in the way of our happiness. Indeed, there was nothing – apart from my illness, which took on new and ever more frightening forms with every passing day. It worsened after my mother's death, only to culminate in my breakdown on the day of Hedvige's funeral. This turned out to be just the first in a series of breakdowns which ultimately led me to this hospital, here in the Alps.

They came on fast: first I'd have an attack of vertigo, then a terrible pain in my head, and next I'd black out. I'd wake up in a bed at the casualty ward where they'd rushed me from the library, the park or the street where I'd collapsed with inhuman cries, they told me. I'd seen a rapid flux of sights, places and epochs tied together into a story whose connecting thread I was unable to apprehend, and that seems to have literally driven me mad. Sequences of historical events alternated with the sequences of stories of those who saw history from the side, askance – its victims. From the beaches of Normandy to Petrograd, from medieval abbeys to the glass-and-steel towers of multinational corporations, a story unfolded in my mind, imperceptibly fast and incomprehensibly complex, but one grand story; and whenever I felt I was finally so close, just one proverbial step away from decoding what at first looked like a chaos of random threads of information, I'd stumble and seize up, drowning in merciful nothingness, with my body sinking in behind.

As if that wasn't enough, the pangs of remorse became more frequent and abrupt. To defend myself from those feelings of guilt would have aroused an even stronger sense of remorse in me because I considered my condition rightful punishment, and evading that punishment seemed unforgiveable. It all climaxed one day when I ordered my favourite roast duck at the Amarcord . . . and then realised I couldn't live a second longer in a world kept in motion only by death. I was inundated with images of hundreds of millions of feathered animals lying on conveyer belts and having their heads sliced off by razor-sharp precision machines. Their cries – through which I clearly discerned the triumphant, self-contented tones of a Black Mass – stabbed into my mind like steely knives. Billions of chicken's legs jerking in their death throes grated at my brain. Cows' heads were severed from their bodies and blood gushed from the necks, bespattering the faces of rubber-suited figures that dragged the carcasses down endless slaughterhouse corridors. Pigs grazed on vast pastures by the sea, only to throw themselves off the cliff one after another, as if at some invisible sign. Lambs were separated from their mothers, whose skulls were then crushed with sledgehammers, and the little animals were herded from their pens to a tract fenced in with barbed wire. There they were gassed to death and mountains of their bodies shifted by bulldozer to restaurants and cafés

120

for our consumption. The thought about how much death was needed to maintain just one human life, my life, made me bolt from the restaurant like a wayward maniac. They didn't find me until evening – wandering aimlessly through the marshes of Lobau.

Marushka will never forgive me for the choice I made. I know she searched for me in all the hospitals in Austria, but I'd covered my tracks. I'd reached the end; she has to keep going. But she can only keep going if she forgets me and forsakes me. I know what she'd wish: to care for me and give me more and more of her unconditional, almost maternal love, the worse my condition became. That would cure me, she believed. She'd lay her life at the altar of my illness. But I can't bear a single sacrifice more for my sake. Instead, I decided to erase myself from her life and liberate her from me. I divided my inheritance into two trusts: one which I manage and use to pay for my luxurious confinement here with a view of the willows and the lake, and a second, which she'll manage when her children are born. That's the closest I'll ever get to fatherhood. I realised that during the first of our fruitless attempts at physical love. Each and every one of them ended in my complete incapacitation, such that we ultimately gave up. I'll never be capable of giving life – but at least I can give money and all that money can buy.

When my mother died, Hedvige handed me a slim book bound in red leather, which she announced as *my mother's diary*. And, in a way which had become habitual, she added in a conspirative-cum-demanding tone: 'This has to stay between us.' My mother turned out to have kept this diary in the period between the separation from you – forgive me for being so direct – and her marriage to the man who would play the role of my father through until the end as well as could be expected under the circumstances. The diary told me nothing about my mother I didn't already know. They never concealed from me that *papa* wasn't my father – a fact underscored multiple times in the diary. But it did reveal the greatest secret: the name of my real father. First you withheld it from me, then my mother; I doubt that *papa* was involved in the decision, although he's sure to have gone along with it in his good-natured way, as with everything else my mother insisted on. Now, thanks to Hedvige, it's become my most precious possession. You may take the mails you're receiving from me as interest on the value you've renounced but which I, nevertheless, will duly reimburse.

PS
We'll see each other soon. At last, I'm coming. Dr Schulz has approved my visit to you: he considers it could be of the greatest significance for my recovery.

Chapter Nine

which tells of an ugly awakening, the devastating power of sincerity, the End which has not come, and the heralding of a long-awaited advent

I woke up in the cold amid a vile stench. I'd vomited in my sleep and made an absolute mess in the car. Before I'd gone to sleep I'd started the motor and turned on the heating, determined not to go home. The fuel ran out during the night and the motor died. Fortunately, some whisky shimmered yellow at the bottom of the bottle.

The snow kept falling. The streets were still empty. Everything just went on: the story about the End concluded like so many others. My head was heavy and still ringing with last night's confessions. Never again would the penitents be able to stand in front of each other. They wouldn't be honest with one another or themselves. Even if they went out drinking together again, nothing would ever be the same. Everything they'd once buried had now risen up out of the deepest dark, the densest forest and the thickest ice to plague them. How many love affairs, friendships and families were destroyed in one moment of nightly candour . . . How many secrets of the dead were released into the world to rob the living of their peace . . . How many husbands and wives are sitting at opposite ends of the cold kitchen table this morning and staring into their steaming cups of coffee because they no longer have the strength to look each other in the eyes . . . How many sons and daughters are staying in their rooms this morning because they don't dare to face up to their parents . . . How empty the confessionals in the churches are this morning after the whole planet turned into one big confessional last night . . . yet in the churches, the truth was spoken in such a way that it remained secret: the priest heard it under oath that he'd keep it confidential, and this prevented it from becoming public and destructive.

The non-occurrence of the catastrophe was a catastrophe which ultimately made the world impossible to live in. The Apocalypse had been a kind of solution, after all. The truth was an incident people had waited for: a comet colliding with the earth, a wave inundating the land, a bomb destroying a tower . . . One drop of the truth and this world became impossible.

The truth is that I 'fathered' him and then deserted him, albeit unwittingly. He ended up in a mental hospital. And even while confined there, he sought my help in vain. He didn't receive a single word from me, nothing but the address to which he could send letters of confession. He won't receive absolution for the sins he committed and the confessions he made to the one whose sin he is.

People are born as sin, a product of sin, and their whole life is a struggle against sinfulness. Sin is unavoidable and undeniable, and the only means of correction people have is death. Yet they consider that if they produce more life they'll help fill the gaping hole in front of them – a hole they don't know what to do about except to learn to ignore it, if they can't manage to plug it in some way. That's why people have children in an ultimate egoistic act, as if it was going to fulfil their life. They cast their children into new emptinesses in an attempt to cover up their own. Then they're overcome by worry, which they think will redeem them. And so the tragedy goes on without end, and generations are sacrificed in vain because their birth was a blunder which rectified nothing. So many generations, so much reproduction – and not the slightest change. Only the same human drama which has been played from the first day on, a play which remains the same old tragicomedy however much scenery and technology is put on stage, however many actors and supernumeraries are involved.

The power to give life is far more destructive and sinister than the power to take away life. Every living creature has that power, however dirty, ugly and stupid it may be. Every father is a father because he was unable to withstand that power. His child will foot the bill for that paternal potency until the end of its days.

In the end, to top it all off, you're stricken with remorse. I have nothing to say to my son other than: I'm sorry. But everyone is always sorry. He's sorry too. Instead of feeling anger because of *what they did to us*, we end up feeling guilty for *what we've done* because we unfailingly feel that our inherent nature is even more corrupt than the circumstances we were born in.

He sent a letter, and with the letter the snow came. His breath has found a way into all the fortresses I had built around me, and crept in beneath all my locked doors. He has followed me like a bloodhound down all the paths I've fled.

What else can I do now but end my flight: to turn around and meet him face to face, like facing a mirror? What can I do now but look down the road and wait, even today, *especially today*, when all flights have been cancelled and the trains and buses are stranded in snowdrifts?

And an anger rose up inside me like a storm surge, like a black ocean pounding down on my chest. I opened the side window, shook out all the heart pills and threw the jar into the snow. Taking a big swig of whisky, I pressed myself back into the seat and my numb hands gripped the steering wheel. I breathed with difficulty. The pain became unbearable – my chest felt like it'd burst open any second and *a stranger* would spring out into the world. I shut my eyes: now I just needed to wait. There was a rushing sound that seemed to be coming from afar, coming ever closer. I wasn't sure if it was the bus Emmanuel was coming with, the final storm which would flatten everything along with the tidal wave which would immerse us all, or my blood seething. Come, I thought. Yes, come.

Soundtrack for *The Coming*

Tilly and the Wall – *Nights of the Living Dead*
R.E.M. – *It's the End of the World as We Know It*
The Clash – *London Calling*
Bat for Lashes – *The Big Sleep*
Sex Pistols – *God Save the Queen*
Nick Cave – *Jesus of the Moon*
Cut City – *Just Pornography*
The Smiths – *Meat is Murder*
The Stone Roses – *Made of Stone*
The Jesus and Mary Chain – *Darklands*
Begushkin – *Bitter Night Choir*
Odawas – *Alleluia*
The Twilight Sad – *Three Seconds of Dead Air*
Belle & Sebastian – *O Come, O Come Emmanuel*

Istros Books

was founded in 2010 with the aim of promoting literature
from South-East Europe in the English-speaking market

Forthcoming titles in 2012

Our Man in Iraq by Robert Perišić

A local journalist sends a distant relative to report on the war in Iraq, while
he stays at home to sort out his love-life and his professional career – all
with varying degrees of success. But as time goes on, things begin to unravel
and he ends up having to fake his missing cousin's reports while struggling
to hold on to his actress girlfriend. *Our Man in Iraq* is a take on the Iraqi
conflict from the other side of Europe, where politics and nepotism collide
and the confusing after-effects of the recent Yugoslav wars mix with the joys
and trials of modern life.

Nine Rabbits by Virginia Zaharieva

Nine Rabbits is a novel in two parts. In the beginning, we meet little Manda, growing up during the height of socialism in Bulgaria in the 1960s,
raised by her tyrannical grandmother. In the second part, forty years later,
that same child has become a woman, now living in democratic times and
racked by an identity crisis. Manda has swallowed up her tyrannical grandmother, turning that despotism against herself. In the heroine's difficult
process of awakening, every shattering of childhood matrices frees up space
for spontaneity, creativity and love. For Manda, the world gradually trans-
forms into a Divine Kitchen, where out of a mixture of characters, places,
ingredients and situations she creates delicious dishes.

Sun Alley by Cecilia Ştefănescu

One summer afternoon, as the twelve-year-old Sal is on his way to see his girlfriend Emi, he is caught in a rain shower and shelters in the hallway of a block of flats. Led by a strong odour, he goes down into the basement, where he comes upon the corpse of a young and very beautiful woman. Little by little, as Sal attempts to discover the mystery of this dead body, the love between the two children blossoms. Yet the secret and malicious adult world threatens to ruin their tender relationship. It seems that the connections between adults and the two children on the one hand, and the dead body discovered by Sal on the other, are much deeper and more complicated than they at first seem. *Sun Alley* is a novel about the roots of adultery and about the destiny of an exceptional young boy.